# "They're playing our tune." Liam gestured to the dance floor. "Shall we?"

Dance? To the song she'd messed up? "I'm not dressed for dancing," she said. Her black trousers and black long-sleeved top were hardly dressy enough to go out for a drink, let alone anything else.

"It doesn't matter. Nobody's watching."

He was right. It didn't matter—not like tonight's performance. So she let him lead her out onto the floor. Stood in hold with him. Let him guide her around the tiny dance floor. Sang along to the words.

And he was smiling as they danced. Not a mocking smile—a real, genuine smile. As if he was enjoying her company. Enjoying the dance.

So was she.

Because here, away from the spotlights and the judges, it worked. The floating feeling was back. She wasn't scared that she'd miss a step, because it really didn't matter if she did. This wasn't for show. It was just for them. For fun.

There were other couples on the dance floor, but she barely noticed them. All she could focus on was Liam. She was shockingly aware of how close he was to her, and how his legs slid between hers and hers slid between his as they turned. He was holding her so close that she could actually feel the heat of his body. And at the end of the dance, when he spun her out in a twirl and then back into his arms, holding her closer still, her heart skipped a beat.

Dear Reader,

This is a special book for me, as it's my very first Harlequin
Romance novel, and I'm so thrilled to have joined the line.
Readers of my Harlequin Presents and Harlequin Medical
Romance books always mention the warmth of my voice when
they write to me, so this series really feels like home.

It's also special because I managed to talk my husband into
being my research assistant for this one. I've always enjoyed
watching ballroom dancing TV shows. When I first thought
about writing this book I discovered that a brand-new
beginners' class was being set up locally. We joined the class so
I could get an idea of what it was like for my heroine, learning
to dance. It's been enormous fun, and we're still going to
classes—it's lovely being whirled around a dance floor!

I also couldn't resist setting part of the story in Vienna, because
we had a fabulous family trip there and it's a beautiful, beautiful
city. (No dancing. But we did have to try pastries, listen to
street musicians and take a trip in a horse-drawn carriage—all
for research purposes, though not all of it ended up here!)

This is a story about second chances and how love can change
everything. Polly is bright and bouncy and happy, but she's
hiding a tragic past; Liam is much more guarded because he
had everything, lost the lot and is putting his life back together
again. Liam teaches Polly to dance, but they teach each other a
much more important lesson: how to love.

I'm always delighted to hear from readers, so do come and visit
me at www.katehardy.com.

With love,

Kate Hardy

# KATE HARDY

*Ballroom to Bride and Groom*

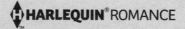

Recycling programs
for this product may
not exist in your area.

ISBN-13: 978-0-373-74231-8

BALLROOM TO BRIDE AND GROOM

First North American Publication 2013

This edition published by arrangement with Harlequin Books S.A.

For questions and comments about the quality of this book, please contact us at CustomerService@Harlequin.com.

® and TM are trademarks of Harlequin Enterprises Limited or its corporate affiliates. Trademarks indicated with ® are registered in the United States Patent and Trademark Office, the Canadian Trade Marks Office and in other countries.

Printed in U.S.A.

**Kate Hardy** lives in Norwich, in the east of England, with her husband, two young children, one bouncy spaniel and too many books to count. When she's not busy writing romance or researching local history she helps out at her children's schools. She also loves cooking—spot the recipes sneaked into her books! (They're also on her website, along with extracts and stories behind the books.) Writing for Harlequin has been a dream come true for Kate—something she has wanted to do ever since she was twelve. She's been writing Medical Romance novels for nearly five years now, and also writes for Presents. She says it's the best of both worlds, because she gets to learn lots of new things when she's researching the background to a book: add a touch of passion, drama and danger, a new gorgeous hero every time, and it's the perfect job!

Kate's always delighted to hear from readers, so do drop in to her website at www.katehardy.com.

**Other titles by this author available in ebook format.**

For Anna and Sheila, my wonderful editors—and for my cheer squad (you know who you are)—with heartfelt thanks for having more faith in me than I did. xxx

# CHAPTER ONE

'POLLY, I know you said you were fine, but I was passing anyway, and I thought I'd just drop in and—' Shona did a double take and stopped short. 'What happened to your hair?'

'I cut it last night.' With nail scissors. The long, straight blonde hair Harry had said he loved was no more. And at least getting rid of it had been Polly's choice. Something that was under her control.

'Cut? Hacked, more like. Has Fliss seen it?'

'Um, no.' And Polly knew her best friend would panic, remembering what Polly had done half a lifetime ago. Her lowest point, when she'd sworn that her life would be perfect from then on, no matter how hard she had to work at it. When she'd learned to smile her way through absolutely anything.

Shona blew out a breath. 'We need to get you to the hairdresser's. Like now.'

Polly waved a dismissive hand. 'I'm fine. It's not as if anyone's going to see me. I don't have to go in to the studio.'

'That, sweetie, is where you're wrong. Coffee, first,' Shona said crisply. 'And, while I'm making it, you need to get changed. The sort of stuff you wore for *Monday Mash-up* will be just fine.'

'I don't work on *Monday Mash-up* any more.' Polly shrugged. 'Anyway, I'm busy.'

'Doing things that Harry really ought to be doing, since he was the one who called off the wedding,' Shona said, her mouth thinning.

'I'm the one who organised it, so it's easier for me to do it. I have the contacts,' Polly pointed out.

She left unsaid what they were both thinking: it also meant that Grace wouldn't be involved. Cancelling the wedding arrangements less than two weeks before the big day was tough enough; letting her ex-fiancé's new girlfriend do it would be just too much to bear. And she knew that Harry would definitely delegate cancelling everything: he'd give that little-boy-lost look that always got him his own way.

'I could strangle Harry, I really could. Selfish doesn't even begin to—' Shona stopped. 'But you already know what I think. OK. Go and get changed while I sort the coffee and make that hair appointment. Oh, and put some stuff under your eyes.'

To cover up the shadows Polly knew were there. It was one of the disadvantages of having fair skin; even one night without sleep meant she had dark shadows under her eyes. She hadn't slept for several, since Harry had told her that he couldn't marry her.

'I do love you, Pol, but…'

As he said the words, someone filled her veins with liquid nitrogen. Freezing her.

*But.*

That meant Harry didn't love her at all.

'…it's as a friend. There just isn't the kaboom,' he finished.

'Kaboom?' She didn't have a clue what he was talking about. How was this happening? Was she in some parallel universe?

'Kaboom. When you meet someone and it's like the sky's full of fireworks.' He gestured wildly, mimicking starbursts in the sky. 'A thousand red balloons floating into the sky.'

She still didn't have a clue what he meant. When she saw Harry, she didn't see dangerous fireworks or balloons that could pop and leave her with nothing. She saw warm and safe and secure. And she'd been so sure he'd felt the same. That they'd be together for ever. That theirs would be one of the marriages people looked up to in showbiz—one that lasted, instead of being over almost as soon as the publicity photos had been printed. Because she and Harry were friends. They fitted. Polly wasn't going to have the same kind of on-again, off-again relationship that her parents had, in between their affairs. This would be a proper marriage. Harry's family liked her. His friends liked her. And her friends liked Harry and his easy charm.

They were a *couple*.

Except now it seemed that they weren't. And her head couldn't process it.

'I'm sorry, Pol.'

And then Harry told her about Grace.

His new assistant, who'd made him feel the kaboom—the way Polly never had…

Polly shook herself and changed into one of the bright long-sleeved T-shirts, jeans and trainers she'd worn on *Monday Mash-up*, then swiftly added enough make-up to erase the shadows and the pallor from her face. And then she pinned on her brightest smile, ready to face the world. By the time she'd finished, Shona had made them both a coffee and was speaking rapidly into the phone.

'I've managed to get you in with Enrique in twenty minutes,' she said. 'I've told him it's urgent. And we'll take a taxi to make sure we get to the studio in time.'

'Which studio?' Polly asked. 'And in time for what?'

Shona shoved one of the mugs towards her. 'Drink this. I put enough cold water in it so you can chug it straight down. I need you awake. Because, sweetie, you're going to be on *Ballroom Glitz*. Starting tomorrow!'

This was definitely a parallel universe. Polly had just walked out of a steady job, knowing that there was a recession on and she'd be lucky to find a waitressing job to tide her over until her agent managed to get her so much as an audition, let alone find something she'd enjoy as much as she'd loved her role as a children's TV presenter. And now Shona was talking about a new contract on a new show? She couldn't quite take it in.

'*Ballroom Glitz*? Since when?'

'Since I got a phone call from the producer an hour ago saying that someone had had to drop out and asking if I had anyone on my books who could fill the slot,' Shona explained. 'Obviously there are other people auditioning for it—but you're going to be the one who gets it, Pol.'

Polly appreciated the older woman's faith in her—right now, her faith in herself was pretty shaky—but she knew it was misplaced. 'Shona, I've got two left feet. Look at the mess I made of it when Danny tried to teach me those dance moves on the show.'

Shona rolled her eyes. 'Danny's not as experienced in teaching as the guys on *Ballroom Glitz* are. And street dance isn't the same as ballroom. You're going to be great.' She patted Polly's shoulder. 'And if you trip or make mistakes, so what? It shows you're real. People will be able to identify with you, Polly.'

Polly couldn't help smiling. 'I'm hardly an A-lister, Shona. *Monday Mash-up* isn't even on terrestrial telly. Nobody's going to have a clue who I am.'

'People like you. They identify with you, and Fliss would tell you the same.'

'Fliss is my best friend. She's supposed to say things like that.'

'It's still true,' Shona said firmly. 'That's why the "Challenge Polly Anna" segment was so popular on *Monday Mash-up*. You did the things people wanted to try doing themselves. And you didn't always beat the challenge—so they knew it was true to life, not something set up with all the flaws airbrushed out. You're going to learn to dance with one of the professionals, and every woman in the country, young or old, will be able to imagine themselves in your shoes. They'll love your warmth and that amazing smile of yours. And *that*, sweetie, is exactly why you're going to nail this audition and be on the show.'

'What about the costumes?' Polly asked quietly. 'They let me have long sleeves on *Monday Mash-up*.'

'They can do the same thing on *Ballroom Glitz*. If not long sleeves, then cuffs or fingerless elbow-length gloves,' Shona reassured her. 'Nobody needs to see your wrists and nobody's going to ask questions. Don't worry.'

Easier said than done. Polly dreaded the wardrobe department seeing her wrists and asking questions—or, worse, speculating. Especially if they thought the scars were because of Harry. Which they weren't.

But being on the show could make a huge difference to her life. It'd mean eight whole weeks of work, if she managed to stay in the competition until the finals. Even if she was voted out at the first elimination, it still meant that she'd have two slots of prime-time exposure—slots that could lead to other opportunities. Plus dancing was something physical that might just tire her out enough to let her sleep in her new flat instead of lying awake and realising how wide the bed seemed without Harry in it, wondering where she'd gone so badly wrong and why she hadn't been enough for him. And she'd have to concentrate on the training, so she wouldn't have time to think about the wreck of her life.

Everything could be perfect again. Far, far away from the lowest point in her life all those years ago. The point that had led to her scars and the long, slow climb to the settled and happy life she'd wanted so badly.

Yeah. She could smile her way through this. *Fake it until you make it.*

'I've always wanted to learn to dance,' Polly said. She pushed away the memories of her five-year-old self begging for ballet lessons and her father's sneered refusal. *Fairy ballerina? Fairy elephant, more like. You're too clumsy, Polly.*

She lifted her chin. 'We've got the lemons. Let's

go make lemonade. With a sparkly swizzle stick in it.'

Shona patted her shoulder. 'Attagirl.'

Six hours later, Polly was back in her flat, making a list of the last few things she needed to cancel for the wedding and answering concerned emails from friends with the minimum of details. Even if she didn't get the *Ballroom Glitz* job, at least she had great hair. Enrique had somehow managed to transform Polly's appalling scissor-job into an urchin cut that made her look like a blonde Audrey Hepburn, all eyes. And in any case the audition had been good practice, reminding her of the skills she needed to brush up on for the future. Today had been a *good* day. And Polly Anna Adams had spent half a lifetime living up to her name. The tougher the going, the brighter her smile. She'd learned to look on the bright side and ignore the difficult stuff. And the strategy *worked*.

All the same, when the phone rang, she let it go through to the answering machine. She wasn't in the mood for sympathy, no matter how well-meaning. Dwelling on things and crying about it wasn't going to make Harry change his mind. Or make her feel better.

'Sweetie, I know you're there. Pick up,' Shona said.

Polly didn't.

There was a sigh. 'All right, do it your way. But I'll be over at ten tomorrow to drag you off to the wardrobe department at the studio. Because you, my clever girl, got the job.'

Polly sat down as the news sank in.

She'd got the job. On *Ballroom Glitz*.

And, although one door had slammed very firmly in her face, another one felt as if it had just opened. One that could lead her to a whole new world.

'See you at ten. And have the kettle on,' Shona said, and hung up.

Two years. How the world could change in two years. Even in one, Liam thought. This time last year, he'd lost everything. His career, his marriage, his home, his dreams. All the experts had said he'd never dance again. But he'd fought to prove them all wrong. Even when his body was screaming for him to stop, he'd pushed himself that little bit further each time, until he could walk again. Until he could dance again.

Every second of agony had been worth it, because now he was back on *Ballroom Glitz*, teaching celebrities to dance on the show and choreographing the routines for the professional dancers. Getting his name back out there.

It still rankled that he had to prove himself all over again, but moaning about it wouldn't get him back to the top. Only sheer hard work would do that.

He just needed to focus and remember the lesson burned into his heart: the only person he could rely on was himself.

Thankfully Bianca wasn't one of the female professional dancers on the team, so that was one less reminder of the past. Half the professional dancers were new, people he hadn't come across before as part of his job; those he did know and had worked with before had given him lots of sympathetic glances, but to his relief they hadn't said anything about the accident or the wreck of his marriage. They'd simply welcomed him back.

So which of the four celebs was going to be his partner? The comedienne wasn't particularly light on her feet, which would mean he'd need to be very careful with any lifts; he really couldn't afford any more damage to his back. Plus her wisecracks seemed to be constant; he could do without that kind of irritation. He wanted someone who'd take this seriously. Someone who'd be prepared to put in the hours it'd take to make them win. The model and the pop singer both moved well—as he'd expect, given their career choices—but both had a hardness about them that reminded him of the worst moments with Bianca.

Which left Polly Anna, the children's TV presenter. Something about her drew him; though, from the video clips the presenter had shown of Polly's show, that was a pretty severe—and very recent—change in haircut. In Liam's experience, when women made a change that radical to their appearance, it meant they were upset about something. *Really* upset. That might affect Polly's ability to concentrate on the choreography. Which didn't bode well for their chances of staying in the show.

He'd just have to make the best of whoever he was teamed with. He put on a smile for the cameras as the runner cued him in, and headed out to the dance floor for the final showcase dance with the other professionals before the pairings were announced.

Which of the four male professionals would be working with her?

Polly had already talked it over with Shona and Fliss. Two of the male dancers were new, making them unknown quantities. André had been part of the show for years, but he'd always come across as a bit strict and humourless in the videos of the training sessions. Definitely not the kind of guy she'd enjoy working with.

And that left Liam Flynn.

Liam, the one she'd always liked most when she'd watched the show in the past. He'd always come across as a really nice guy, supportive and kind to his dancing partner. Plus he was very, very easy on the eyes: tall, dark and utterly gorgeous.

Except Liam had been in a serious car accident eighteen months ago, and at the time the media had claimed he'd never be able to dance again. Clearly he'd had a lot of physical therapy to get him back to this point. And, although Liam was the dancer she'd love to be teamed with, Polly couldn't help worrying. She knew she was clumsy. What if she tripped and they fell awkwardly, and that hurt his back again, and this time his dancing was over for good?

She damped down the fears. No. She was going to work hard. She was going to beat the clumsiness. And she most definitely wasn't going to let what had happened with Harry shred her confidence. She'd been totally professional and given her best on *Monday Mash-up*, and she'd do exactly the same on *Ballroom Glitz*.

'And now the moment you've been waiting for— the official line-up,' Millie, the glamorous presenter of the show, announced.

There was a drum roll while the dancers stood on the floor, waiting for their partners to join them, and the celebs lined the staircase.

*You're not going to trip*, Polly told herself firmly. *You're not going to trip. Take it step by step. Remember to smile for the cameras.*

She barely took in which male celebrity was paired with which female dancer. She felt like a rabbit caught in the headlights. But then it came to the girls, and her hands went clammy.

'And with André...' *Please, please, not me*, she begged silently.

She breathed a sigh of relief as Jane, the comedienne, was announced as his partner. Mr No-Sense-of-Humour with the comic: the pairing appealed to Polly's sense of mischief. It was exactly what she would've done, as a producer. What Harry would've done.

*Forget about Harry*, she reminded herself sharply. *He isn't here and he isn't part of your life any more.*

'With Marco...' Imogen, the model. They made a beautiful couple.

'With Sergei...' Her heart skipped a beat. Would it be her?

'Lina.' The pop singer. Another glamorous, beautiful couple. Which meant...

'And finally, with Liam, Polly Anna Adams.'

She walked down the stairs, smiling for the cameras, and walked over to Liam as everyone applauded.

Wow. That gorgeous smile she'd seen on the small screen was even more devastating in the flesh. Liam Flynn was stunning. His skin was very pale, in sharp contrast to his dark hair, and there was a light sprinkling of stubble on his cheeks that made her itch to reach out and trail her fingertips across it.

Not that she'd do that. Especially in front of the cameras. She wasn't going to make a fool of herself.

But he had a beautiful mouth. Full, generous—lush.

And his eyes were almost navy blue. With his colouring, they were absolutely mesmerising.

She bit her lip, hoping that he hadn't noticed her giving him the eye. And what on earth was she doing, having thoughts like this about another man merely a week before her wedding-day-that-wasn't? Clearly she was letting the roar of the crowd and the glitziness of the lights get to her.

She shook herself. Be professional. That was what she had to do. And do it *now*.

Polly Anna Adams was much prettier in the flesh than she'd been in the video clips, with huge eyes, a heart-shaped face and a perfect rosebud mouth that just invited Liam to rub his thumb along her lower lip.

Though he had no intention of giving in to the mad temptation. This was strictly business. And he didn't do involvement on any level, any more. Not since Bianca. He'd learned the hard way that he was better off on his own. Besides, he didn't have the time. He had a business to set up and a career to get back on track.

He dutifully kissed Polly's cheeks for the audience, and caught her scent. Light, floral with a hint of vanilla. Sweet and innocent. Nothing like the sultry, spicy scent that Bianca had used.

She reminded him of Audrey Hepburn, with that urchin haircut and those huge chocolate-brown eyes.

The wardrobe department had obviously clocked that, too, giving her a simple black shift dress teamed with long silky gloves, a pearl choker, and classic high-heeled court shoes. The outfit wasn't like the eye-wincingly bright clothes Polly Anna had worn in the video clips—of course not, because she needed casual clothing to do all the mad stuff with the kids on *Monday Mash-up*—but it suited her down to the ground. Glamorous, graceful...

And then she slipped on those high, high heels as she turned to face the audience.

Scratch graceful, he thought wryly.

Automatically, he caught her and steadied her.

'Thanks,' she mouthed, and her blush was visible right through the studio pan stick. 'And sorry.'

But the audience weren't laughing at the unintended slapstick. They were clapping even more. Because she'd shown that she was human, just like them: not some impossibly glamorous model or pop star they could only be like in their dreams.

Once the show was off air and they were heading back towards the Green Room, Polly bit her lip. 'I'm really sorry about that. I'm not used to walking in heels.'

Or dancing, Liam thought, but he couldn't quite be unkind enough to say so. 'Tomorrow's Sunday. Are you OK to start training then, or do you need to be in rehearsals for your show?'

'I'm—I guess you'd say *resting*, right now,' she admitted, looking awkward.

Showbiz-speak for unemployed. Which gave her a real motivation for staying in the competition.

'I can fit training sessions around whatever suits you. If I get any auditions, I should be able to give you at least a day's notice,' she finished.

'Good. Lark or owl?'

She blinked. 'I'm sorry?'

Lord, her eyes were gorgeous. He could drown in them.

He pushed the thought away. For pity's sake. He needed to concentrate on doing his job, not let himself get distracted by a pretty face. Hadn't he learned a thing from his past? 'Are you better working earlier or later in the day?'

'Oh. I'm a morning person. As long as I've had a cup of coffee, first.' She gave him what he thought might be the first real smile he'd seen from her, one that put a dimple in her cheek and a sparkle in those huge eyes. A smile that made him catch his breath.

'Fine. I'll see you tomorrow at eight, then, at my studio.' He handed her a business card, and his skin tingled where his fingers brushed against hers. Which was insane: he couldn't afford to let himself get distracted. 'My mobile number's on the back, in case you're going to be late or can't make it.'

'Thank you. I'm sorry, I don't have a business

card with me, but I'll text you on the way home so you have my number,' she said.

'Fine. See you at eight, then,' Liam said. And then he left abruptly, before he let himself do something totally stupid. Like wondering if her lips were as soft and as sweet as they looked. And then being tempted to dip his head to find out...

# CHAPTER TWO

Liam glanced at his watch when the studio's entry-system intercom buzzed the next morning. Five to eight. Polly Anna was actually on time.

He'd always had to give Bianca a fake deadline two hours earlier than the real one, to give them a hope of being on time—whether it was work or a social event—and it had driven him crazy.

At least Polly Anna was sparing him that. So far.

'Hello? It's Polly Anna Adams, here for training with Mr Flynn.'

'Let's drop the formalities. I'm Liam,' he said. 'I'll buzz you in. The studio's on the third floor.'

He waited in the reception area for her to walk up the two flights of stairs. As she emerged through the door, she caught her bag on the door handle, and the door banged against her.

Her face went crimson. 'I'm so sorry, Mr Fl— Liam,' she corrected herself.

Impatience warred with being charmed. Charmed won. Just. 'It's fine, Polly Anna. Are you OK?'

She nodded. 'Everyone calls me Polly.'

'Polly. Come through to the studio and we can talk about the training schedule.' He gestured towards the studio door.

He assessed Polly swiftly as she walked across the room. She'd replaced yesterday's glamorous outfit and high heels with loose black trousers and a loose long-sleeved black top, teamed with flat shoes. Despite the camouflage of her clothes, he could see that she didn't have a dancer's physique, and she moved without a dancer's easy grace.

A total beginner, then. He'd need to push her.

'What dancing experience do you have?' he asked.

'None. Except a little bit of street dance on the show,' she admitted, confirming his assessment, 'and I was absolutely hopeless. It's just as well they didn't show that clip on Saturday night.'

Her smile had turned super-bright. Defence mode again, he guessed. He had no idea why, and he wasn't going to ask. 'You must have danced at some point in your life, even if it was just at a wedding.'

Was it his imagination, or did she just flinch?

'I've swayed with someone on a dance floor a couple of times, yes, but that's about it.'

'How about aerobics classes?' Some of them used dance routines.

She shook her head. 'I've never had a gym membership or gone to any kind of class. I'm not really one for exercise, apart from the stuff they got me to do on *Monday Mash-up*,' she admitted. 'I'd much rather curl up on the sofa with a good book or watch a movie.'

Whereas doing something so passive would bore him witless; he was happiest when he was dancing, losing himself in the music and pushing his body to its limits.

She looked awkward. 'You've probably worked out already that I'm a bit clumsy.'

Yes, and part of him found it endearing. But being soft on her wouldn't get the job done. He pushed the thought away. 'Do you sing or play an instrument?'

'No.'

Well, it didn't necessarily mean that she wasn't musical. Maybe she just hadn't had the opportunity to learn to play something. 'OK.' He remembered what she'd said the previous day. 'Do you want a coffee before we start?'

She shook her head. 'Thanks, but I'm already caffeined up.'

He'd just bet she was worrying about spilling her drink. And that smile had turned a little too bright again. He ought to be nice and reassure her. But he'd done his fair share of helping lame ducks in the past, and look where that had got him. Divorced and having to build up his life again from ground zero. He didn't need any more disruption.

Particularly as he couldn't deny that he found

Polly attractive. Those wide eyes. That perfect rose-bud mouth.

Not good. He needed to keep this strictly professional. This was *work*. He took his iPod from his pocket. 'Right, let's start with the basics. I'm going to play you snippets from a few songs, and I want you to tell me if you can hear the beat of the music in each one. Tap it out on your knee or the table, or whatever makes you comfortable. And try to emphasise the strong beat in the bar.'

'The strong beat?' She looked mystified.

He was really going to have his work cut out here. 'The first beat of the bar is the strongest and you'll hear that more easily than anything else. Don't worry about the introduction. Just tap your finger when you feel you can hear a strong beat, and count from that until the next strong beat. You'll hear it as *one*-two-three, or *one*-two-three-four.'

'OK.'

He flicked into the first track, a waltz he'd deliberately chosen to have a clear triple-time beat. When Polly stumbled over tapping out the rhythm and was clearly cross with herself for not being able to do it, he tapped it out for her. 'Can you hear it now?' he asked.

'Sorry,' she said with a grimace. 'Obviously I'm tone-deaf as well as clumsy.'

Yeah. For a moment, Liam wished he'd been paired with the pop singer. At least she would've been able to grasp the basics. Still, he'd been part-nered with Polly and he had to make the best of it. 'Try and listen to as much different music as you can, listen to the beat and practise.'

'Right.'

So far, so bad. He stifled a sigh. 'Ballroom dancing is just following a set pattern of steps and matching them to the music. Let's start with a basic forward and reverse.'

'We're going to dance right now?' She looked horrified.

Just for a second, Liam found himself wanting to reassure her. Polly was very close to getting under his skin. Which rattled him to the point where he found himself being snippy with her, to stop his thoughts going any further in that direction. 'Did you think we'd wait until the morning of the show before we started practising?'

Her face went a dull red. 'No.' She glanced at the sprung wood floor. 'Do I need to take my shoes off?'

'No.' He looked at her flat shoes. 'But if you have some shoes with a slight heel that you can bring with you, next time, you'll find it easier on your calves and ankles.'

'Do I need to wear a skirt?'

'As long as it doesn't restrict your movements, you can wear anything you like.'

\* \* \*

Although she'd worked in TV for long enough to know that most people worked hard to maintain an image for the screen, Polly was still disappointed to realise that Liam Flynn wasn't the sweet, smiling guy he'd always seemed on the show. He was clearly trying to suppress his impatience—OK, so her clumsiness would drive anyone crazy—but he hadn't even tried to put her at ease.

Well, she'd just have to make the best of this. Even if training turned out to be some nightmare boot camp, she needed to stay on the show. She wanted her perfect life back. And *Ballroom Glitz* was the best way to get it.

She gave him her brightest smile. 'So how much time do you think we'll need for training?'

'We'll do four hours today, maybe more tomorrow. Let's see how it goes. Though we'll avoid the evenings. I don't want to cause problems with your partner.'

So he hadn't been that fully briefed about her, then—and he definitely hadn't read the gossip rags, or he'd know that Harry had called off the wedding last weekend. *Celebrity Life* had run a centre spread the previous Thursday entitled 'Poor Polly', showing her looking a wreck and Grace looking utterly stunning.

Well, she wasn't going to bring up the subject of her wedding-that-wasn't. She didn't want Liam's pity. This was her new life, and she wasn't letting any of her old life spill into this one and get in the way. 'I'm single.' She hadn't cried about the break-up yet and she wasn't going to start now. She lifted her chin and gave him another brilliant smile. 'So it isn't a problem.'

'Good. We'll start with the frame. If you watched the show before, you might've heard the judges talk about the "frame".'

'Yes.'

'The frame is what helps me lead you round the dance floor. It means our movements are synchro-nised and in time.' He stood in front of her, both arms bent at the elbow and resting against her sides.

Her pulse kicked up a notch at the contact. Unex-pected, and scary at the same time; she hadn't even reacted physically like this to Harry, and she'd been going to marry him.

Nerves. It had to be nerves, she told herself, and her brain was so scrambled that it was misinterpret-ing her reactions. This wasn't attraction. It couldn't be. She didn't even *like* the man.

'With your left hand, you're going to make a vee with your thumb and middle finger,' he said, 'and you're going to rest that on the vee in my muscles.'

It was suddenly hard to breathe. She was up close and personal with Liam Flynn. On TV, he was gor-geous. In the flesh, he was really something. She'd just have to remember that his charm was only for the cameras. And charm wasn't something she trusted any more. Not after the way Harry had let her down.

'Start at my elbow and push your hand up until you find the vee,' Liam instructed.

And now she was touching him. Running her fingers over his bare skin, because he was wearing a vest-type T-shirt. And every nerve in her body felt as if it had just sat up and begged.

Oh, help. Looking at and appreciating a fine male form was perfectly acceptable—expected, even, in her world—but getting this warm, sensual coil of desire in her belly... That was scary. Not what she needed or wanted right now.

And it made her cross with herself. She was being pathetic and needy, on the rebound and desperate for some affection from anyone who was in the slightest bit kind to her—and Liam hadn't exactly been kind. He hadn't even so much as smiled at her.

'I've found the vee,' she said.

'Now lift your third and index fingers up as if they're a butterfly's wings,' he said.

She was all too aware of the narrow band of white on her left ring finger, but he made no comment.

'Now, your right hand.' He moved his left arm, pivoting from the elbow, so that his palm was facing her and his thumb was lifted. 'Sometimes you see people dancing with their fingers laced together. It doesn't work in ballroom, because when you want to do a turn you'll end up in a tangle if your fingers are linked. So instead you rest your fingers over mine, and curve your thumb round mine, so you can turn your hand in mine when you need to.' He talked her through the hold.

He really hadn't been prepared for the touch of her skin against his. How it would make him feel. That it would make him want to slip out of the ballroom hold and tangle his fingers properly with hers.

This was supposed to be work. He really shouldn't be letting himself get so distracted by her. *Attracted* by her.

Annoyance at his reaction to her made him sharp. 'And that's it.'

Except now she had to move her feet. Which might be a problem.

'OK. Now the feet.' He dropped her hands. 'One small step back with your right foot.' He blew out a breath as she took a step back with her left foot. 'Your *right* foot, Polly.'

'Is it any wonder I can't tell my right from my left, when you're glaring at me like that?' She shook her head. 'I thought you'd be different.'

He frowned. 'How do you mean?'

'Maybe I've been spoiled, because the boys on *Monday Mash-up* are the same offscreen as they are onscreen. But you're not. I used to watch *Ballroom Glitz* and you were *nice*. Supportive.'

Liam lifted his chin. 'I am being supportive.'

'Right,' she scoffed. 'You haven't said a single encouraging word to me.'

'What do you want me to do? Tell you how marvellous you are while you're doing something wrong? That's not going to help you improve, is it?'

'No, but it wouldn't kill you to smile.'

'Says the woman who smiles all the time and pretends everything's perfect.'

It wasn't pretend. If she tried hard enough, it became real. 'Haven't you ever heard the saying, "smile and the world smiles with you"?'

'It's fake.'

'Fake it until you make it,' Polly said. 'Don't knock it. It works.'

He rolled his eyes. 'I need you to concentrate on learning these steps. I assume you actually want to stay in the competition?'

'I can't afford not to,' she admitted.

'Then concentrate, Polly. Right foot back.'

She narrowed her eyes at him. 'The papers said you were planning to start master-classes on dancing, for actors and what have you.'

He frowned again. 'Yes.'

'I wouldn't bother,' she said. 'Because, the way you are with people, they won't want to come back for a second lesson.'

'Or maybe they'll be professional and concentrate their energies on learning the steps instead of grinning inanely.'

She could walk out of that door, right now.

But the show was her best chance of finding another job and getting her life back to normal. Back to perfect. So walking out wasn't a real option.

She gritted her teeth. 'Just in case it hasn't occurred to you, I *know* I'm massively clumsy. I'm scared I'm going to make a mess of this. And your attitude isn't helping. Here's the deal. You try to be less abrasive, and I'll try harder to do what you tell me and get it right.'

Liam hadn't expected Little Miss Sweetness-and-Light to have that much of a backbone.

Maybe there was more to her than that super-bright smile.

And maybe she had a point. In the past, he'd been kind to his partners on *Ballroom Glitz*, and that had helped him teach them the trickier steps. OK, so he'd been in a different place then, and he was still angry that he had to build his career up from scratch again, but taking out his anger on Polly—particularly because his body's reaction to her threw him—wasn't going to help either of them.

'I'm sorry. I haven't been fair to you,' he said. 'I guess it's daunting if you haven't danced before.'

'Thank you for acknowledging that. And it must be frustrating if the person you're teaching doesn't get it and you think it's because they're not paying attention.'

She understood that? He echoed her words. 'Thank you for acknowledging that.' He looked at her. 'I think we've got off on the wrong foot.'

'Literally.' She smiled at him.

Genuinely, this time. So he made the effort to smile back. 'Shall we start again? And maybe you'll find it easier if we're in hold and I'm leading you.'

'You feel too close,' she said, 'in hold. I'm not used to being that close to someone I barely know.'

And that worried her? Did she think he was going to come on to her? 'Is this where I do the Johnny Castle line about my space and your space?' he asked lightly.

Her eyes crinkled at the corners. 'I love that film. But I'm never going to dance like Baby. If you make me do steps on a tree-trunk, I'll fall off and break my ankle.'

'Firstly, we're sticking to a dance floor. No tree-trunks. Secondly, Baby and Johnny weren't dancing ballroom. And, thirdly, you need to forget what you think you can't do and trust me.'

'I don't know you. How can I trust you?'

Fair point. He didn't trust her, either. He didn't trust anyone. 'What was that you were saying about fake it until you make it?' It came out slightly more caustic than he'd intended, and he felt a throb of guilt when she flinched.

'OK. I'll pretend I trust you.'

'Good. Back in hold, then.' He squeezed her right hand. 'You start with the leg on this side. Your *right*. One step back.'

It was a truce, of sorts. Polly decided to accept it.

'Left leg back the same amount.'

She followed his instructions carefully.

'Now a tiny step to the side with your right leg—' he squeezed her right hand again '—and then bring your left leg across to join it so your feet are together.'

Step, step.

'That's it. You've just done your first basic.'

She coughed.

'What?'

'Well done?' she prompted.

He rolled his eyes. 'Polly, it was four steps. If you want a "well done", you have to earn it.'

She should've expected that. 'Right.'

'And now we're going to do the next one—this time, you're the one who moves forward. Ready? Forward, forward, side, side.' He talked her through it—and it actually worked. She hadn't stood on his toes or tripped. *You need to forget what you think you can't do and trust me.* Maybe he was right. Even if he didn't smile.

'We'll do a forward and a back now, to make a complete set.'

She wasn't sure if she was more surprised or thrilled that she managed eight whole steps without tripping. And it was all thanks to him talking her through it. Being patient. Making more of an effort.

'Now, let's look at the rhythm. It's slow, slow, quick-quick. And it's a lot easier to do it to music, so let me go and sort that out.'

Polly watched Liam walk over to the corner of the room, where a music system was set up. There was something about a dancer's walk: neat, beautiful. She couldn't quite bring herself to use the G-word— not with the connotations that word had for her— but it would describe his movements perfectly. He might be grouchy, but he had style. And how.

He connected his iPod to the system, flicked a switch, and the first few bars of the music flooded into the studio. She didn't have a clue what the beat of the song was. But she was going to have to trust Liam not to let her go wrong.

He took her hand and led her to the far side of the room. 'We're going to do the steps I just taught you, for the whole length of the room,' he said. 'Are you ready?'

She nodded.

'Here we go. Slow, slow, quick-quick; slow, slow, quick-quick.' He talked her through the steps.

And it felt as if she were floating.

She'd never, ever experienced anything like this. And when he guided her effortlessly round the corners and danced her all the way back down the room again…

'Wow,' she said when the song ended. 'I never thought I'd be able to do that.'

At the beginning of their lesson, he'd had his doubts, too. But she'd worked hard. Made the effort. And, from the look of wonder in her eyes, he was pretty sure that she'd just got what he loved about ballroom dancing. OK, it was tiny, as far as breakthroughs went, but it was a start. Part of him wanted to pick her up and spin her round. But the sensible side of him remained in control. Just.

'Told you so,' he said laconically.

'Smugness,' she said, 'is not a good look on you, Mr Flynn.'

It was the first time she'd really answered him back—teasing, confident, and incredibly sweet. Liam couldn't help responding to the glint in her eyes: he smiled at her.

Polly stared at Liam in surprise. It was the first time she'd seen him really smile. A genuine, full-wattage smile that left her knees temporarily weak.

And it flustered her so much that she tripped at the first step of the next song.

'Concentrate, Polly,' he said, the smile gone again. 'We'll keep going until you can do this without having to think about the steps or which leg's which.'

And he meant it. They didn't stop for the next hour.

Then he allowed them a brief break for a late breakfast of a bacon sandwich and a coffee in the café round the corner. Polly spilled the tomato ketchup everywhere, but Liam didn't comment. He just ushered her back to the studio afterwards and made her go through the steps over and over again.

By the end of the session, she wasn't having to think any more about which was her left and which was her right, when to go forward and when to go back.

'We'll stop there for today,' he said at the end of the song.

'Uh-huh.' Polly didn't trust herself to say any more. Just in case her disappointment at his lack of praise showed.

'I'll see you tomorrow. Eight sharp. I'll send you a list of songs this evening. Listen to them, pick the ones you like best and we'll use them in training.'

'OK.'

She was at the door when he said, 'And, Polly?'

She turned to face him, expecting another order.

'Well done.'

It took a moment to sink in, and then Polly wasn't sure whether she wanted to hug him or throttle him. The man was infuriating.

But he'd actually praised her. And, given that he'd told her she'd have to earn it, it meant a lot more than the 'you were marvellous, darling' she was used to hearing in her old job. Not that she'd risk another 'told you so' by admitting that.

'Thank you,' she said. 'See you tomorrow.'

# CHAPTER THREE

LIAM thought about ignoring the phone later that evening, but the caller display showed that it was his PA. He'd better answer, in case she needed tomorrow off or something. 'Yes, Mand. What can I do for you?'

'Are you online?' Amanda asked.

'Yes. Why?'

'There's something I think you need to see. I'm not spreading gossip,' Amanda added swiftly. 'Just… look, Polly Anna's *nice*. My kids love her on *Monday Mash-up*. She's not the sort who whines about breaking a nail or flounces about in a huff—she just gets on with things and does her job with a smile, whatever they throw at her. And, believe you me, they throw some really tough stuff at her.'

'I'd already worked that one out for myself, Mand,' Liam said.

'Go easy on her, that's all. She's having a hard time right now. I mean, I know you've had a hard time, too, thanks to the accident and Bianca, but—'

'I have to teach Polly to dance,' Liam cut in, not wanting to discuss his ex-wife. 'And you saw the video clips.' Polly definitely wasn't afraid of working hard, but her coordination was an issue that could hold them back on the show.

'She's a sweetie, Liam.'

Hmm. If his PA was batting Polly's corner like this, there was a fair chance that a lot of the women who watched *Ballroom Glitz* would be supporting Polly, too. For similar reasons. 'OK.'

'I've emailed you the link. Read the story, but don't tell her you know about it.' Amanda blew out a breath. 'I could punch that Harry, I really could.'

Harry? Who was Harry? 'Right. I'll see you in the morning,' Liam said. 'Polly's going to be in the studio with me from eight.'

'OK. It'll be nice to meet her. See you tomorrow.'

Liam flicked into his email program, followed the link Amanda had sent him to a story on *Celebrity Life* magazine, and read the gossip-page story in silence.

Now he knew why Polly had cut her hair short. And why she had that super-bright smile. And why she'd flinched when he'd mentioned dancing at a wedding: because her engagement to Harry, the producer of her show, had just been broken. Very, very publicly.

Thanks to Bianca, he knew what it felt like to be dumped in the full glare of the public eye. *Celebrity*

*Life* had scooped Bianca's plans before she could tell him that she was leaving him for someone else—a man who could still dance and help her win a World Championship trophy, at the point when everyone had thought that Liam's career was over.

And he'd hated every single one of the pitying smiles that people had given him afterwards. Every single one of the platitudes mouthed at him. They hadn't had a clue how he'd felt. How hurt and angry and resentful. And how relieved, in a weird way: because being brave for Bianca's sake and pretending that he felt just fine had become so, so wearing.

He'd bet it was just the same for Polly. A mixture of misery and anger and all kinds of unwelcome emotions. So, no, he wouldn't tell her that he knew about the break-up. He'd spare her the pity party.

But he wasn't going to go easy on her, either. That wouldn't be doing her any favours; she needed to work hard if she was going to stay in the competition. And staying in the competition, he thought, might just be better for her confidence and her self-esteem than anything else right now.

Polly was outside the dance studio at five to eight the next morning. When she rang the intercom, Liam buzzed her in.

'So, did you like any of the songs I sent you?'

'Yes. But they're a bit—well, old-fashioned. The kind of thing my grandparents would listen to.'

'You'd be surprised at how popular they are among people in their twenties. They're easy to dance to.' He shrugged. 'I have a friend who's a wedding DJ and he sends people to me to choreograph their first dance. Sometimes they have a song in mind; if they don't, that's the list I usually send them.'

*Their first dance.* Polly couldn't help flinching. She could see that Liam noticed, but was grateful that he didn't ask why. Though she had a nasty feeling that someone must've told him. Or maybe he'd seen the story in one of the weekend papers. Not that she'd been able to face looking through them herself, but she was pretty sure they would've run the story about *When Harry Dumped Polly*. Especially as she was in something as high-profile as *Ballroom Glitz*.

She only hoped that the interviewer in *Step by Step*, the Thursday evening programme that followed the couples and their training, wouldn't ask her about it. Because she really, really didn't want to talk about Harry and Grace.

'Right. Time for training. Show me the steps you learned yesterday.'

She took a pair of shoes from her bag and showed them to him. 'Are these OK?'

'As long as they're comfortable, yes.' He gave her a guarded look. 'If you've forgotten the steps, just say. Don't waste time.'

'I haven't forgotten,' she said, giving him another

glower as she changed her shoes. 'There's no need to be snippy with me.'

He said nothing, just raised an eyebrow.

'Right leg back, left leg back, step right to the side, bring both feet together,' she said, talking herself through the sequence. 'Back, back, side, close. Slow, slow, quick-quick.'

'Can you remember the hold?'

'I might be a novice dancer,' she said crisply, 'but credit me with a *little* intelligence. If I can't remember something, I'll ask you.'

He inclined his head but didn't smile or try to mollify her. 'The hold?'

'Left hand, the vee and the butterfly fingers,' she said, doing it. 'Right hand, up and with my fingers over yours and my thumb round yours.'

'Good.' He'd clearly already cued up the music, and this time used a remote control to switch it on. 'Let's go.'

Her skin tingled where it touched his, flustering her into missing a couple of steps. Liam gave her a speaking look.

'Sorry,' she mumbled.

'Let's start again.'

This time, something seemed to click; she was still incredibly aware of his body, his closeness, but this time it meant that her movements dovetailed with his. Connected. Going round the dance floor seemed entirely natural. By the time the music stopped, she felt as if she'd actually achieved something. And she loved that feeling.

'I'll teach you the next step after coffee,' Liam said.

'Not one of the spinning-round steps?' she asked. Right now she couldn't ever see herself being able to manage that.

'Not today. Though you will be doing that pretty soon. And you're talking either about a spot turn or a pivot.'

Polly placed her palm horizontally and whooshed it just above her head. Just so he'd know she didn't have a clue what he was talking about.

'Message received and understood,' he said.

And then he smiled.

There was a funny feeling in the pit of Polly's stomach. Not the same feeling she'd had when Harry smiled at her, all warm and safe; this wasn't safe at all. It was something dangerous. Something she couldn't cope with.

She fell back on her standby—a super-bright smile—and followed him into the kitchen. This time he took three mugs from the cupboard.

'Three mugs?' she asked.

'One's for Amanda,' he explained. 'My PA. She keeps things running for me. Well, part time. She works for me between the school runs.'

As if on cue, a woman with wild, curly red hair walked in. 'He's a slave-driver. My advice would be, don't let him get away with a thing.' She smiled at Polly. 'It's great to meet you, Polly Anna. I'm Amanda. My kids love you on *Monday Mash-up*, so we'd be voting for you even if you weren't dancing with Liam.'

Polly's eyes were stinging, and she blinked back the tears. She wasn't going to start crying just because someone was being kind to her. OK, so she'd miss the team on *Monday Mash-up*—she'd miss them horribly, because Danny, Mike and Charlie had become good friends over the last couple of years—but life had to go on.

Just as long as Harry didn't put Grace in Polly's place on the show, as well as her place in his life.

She lifted her chin, straightened her back and gave Amanda a full megawatt smile. 'Thank you.'

'Pleasure.' Amanda waved a packet of chocolate biscuits at Liam. 'Supplies. And I brought more proper coffee, because I bet you forgot.' She smiled at Polly. 'I'll let you into a secret. Liam has a horribly sweet tooth. If he starts being bossy, just give him cake. Then he'll be nice to you.'

This time, Polly's smile was genuine.

'I like Amanda,' she said when Liam led her back into the dance studio.

'So do I.' He paused. 'And I'm not bossy.'

'You are.'

'No, I'm focused,' he corrected. 'Which is how

I need you to be, right now, because I'm going to teach you the balance step.'

'Balance step,' she repeated. How ironic, for someone as clumsy as her. She was only surprised that nobody had suggested she tried tightrope-walking on the 'Challenge Polly Anna' slot. Or maybe they had, and Harry had nixed it because he hadn't wanted her to fall off and break her neck or something. 'OK. I'm listening.'

'Instead of moving two steps forward or back, we stay where we are and shift our weight—just a gentle side-to-side rock, really—and then we do the side-close.' He talked her through it.

Polly just couldn't get the hang of it and kept swaying the wrong way. Which made things worse, because then she ended up even closer to Liam, physically. Every time she touched him, even through layers of clothes, it made her feel as if the air were crackling round her.

Which was ridiculous.

She barely knew the man. And he wasn't sweet and gentle, the way Harry was. He was driven and intense. Scary. And it threw her when he switched between being Mr Nice for the cameras and Mr Snippy, who only just managed to suppress his impatience with her inability to pick up the steps. Which was the real Liam?

'You're panicking,' Liam said.

Yeah. He could say that again.

'OK. Back to basics. This is exactly the same as we did before, except your feet don't move for the first two steps—you just shift your weight as if you were taking a step to the side and then back again. Right, left, right, close.'

It took her a while, but finally she got the hang of it. And then, without even the hint of a break, he took her through the promenade step. 'We're both going to turn to face the same way, point our arms out together, and step forward. Remember you always move your right foot first, then your left.' He demonstrated. 'Then we turn to face each other again, step right to the side, and close with your left foot.'

Tricky. She had to think about which was her left and which was her right. And she got it wrong half the time.

He sighed. 'Am I going to have to tie ribbons to your wrists, or something? Red for left and white for right?'

No way in hell was he getting close to her wrists. 'There's no point. I'd only get it mixed up with red for right and left for lemon,' she said sweetly.

He muttered something that sounded like, 'Give me strength.'

But eventually Polly got the hang of it. And when she stopped concentrating so hard, she was surprised to discover that she was actually having fun. She loved the music he was playing—an old Van Morrison track with a strong beat that even she could hear clearly—and she was finally moving around the floor with him, so easily that her worries about tripping over him faded into the background.

'I love this,' she said, smiling. 'I totally get why you do this for a living.' She hummed along to the song.

When Liam realised that she'd changed the lyrics to talk through what she was doing—not to guide herself, but almost celebrating the steps—he couldn't help smiling back. 'Yes. It's everything. The music, the steps, how it all blends together and your body's in tune with the whole lot.'

She looked up at him, her brown eyes sparkling with pleasure. At that moment, Liam felt connected with her. *Really* connected. The beat of the music was thrumming through his body, and he knew it was the same for her.

It would be oh, so easy to dip his head, find out if that lush mouth was as soft and sweet as he suspected...

And he'd really need his head examined. This was a complication he didn't want or need. Yes, they could keep dancing, but he needed some space. *Now.* He stopped. 'OK. That's us done for today. See you tomorrow.'

She blinked for a moment, as if she'd lost herself in the dance, then gave him one of her super-bright smiles, making him feel obscurely guilty. 'See you tomorrow,' she echoed.

The next morning, Polly arrived at the studio with a bag of Danish pastries. 'There's a nice bakery round the corner from my flat, and as you're providing the coffee I thought this could be my contribution. I'll leave a note in the kitchen so Amanda knows to help herself, too.' She gave him an arch look. 'Plus the sugar might sweeten your mood so you don't get stroppy with me this morning.'

'Don't push it. We're doing corners this morning. I'll have to be stroppy with you.'

But she did at least get a smile out of him. Score one to Polly Anna, she thought.

Except that smile did things to her. If it weren't so ridiculous, she'd be tempted to think that this was the *kaboom* Harry had described. Her stomach was all fluttery, her skin felt too tight and her temperature was definitely a couple of degrees above normal. Worse still, it made her more aware of him physically. Of how small the gap was between their bodies when they danced. Of how easy it would be to close that gap. Of what it would be like to be skin to skin with him.

And the whole thing sent her into flat spin. It had taken her months to fall for Harry, and even then she hadn't felt a physical reaction towards him like this.

How could she feel this sort of thing about Liam, when she barely knew him?

She really had to get this under control. He was her dancing partner for the show. No way could she let him become anything more than that. Her heart had already been stomped on; and she had no intention of letting anyone near her until she'd got some good, solid defences in place. Defences that would mean nobody could hurt her again, the way that Harry had.

# CHAPTER FOUR

EVERYTHING was fine until Saturday.

*Saturday.*

The day Polly had been trying not to think about.

Liam was busy during the day, so they weren't doing their training session until the evening. And she'd already refused offers to spend time with her friends—even her best friend—because she really didn't want to spend the day brightly talking about anything else except the elephant in the room. Thankfully they'd accepted her excuse that she couldn't make it because she was training. It was true; she'd simply been a little creative with the timing of her session.

She spent the day scrubbing her flat, to keep herself busy. With long rubber gloves that hid her wrists. She wasn't going back *there*. Ever again. She was older and wiser, and she'd learned to focus on the positive side; even if there was one dusty droplet of water in her glass, as far as she was concerned it was still partly full instead of mostly empty. And she had a lot to be thankful for. She had a roof over her head, even if her flat was tiny; she had a job, even if it was a bit precarious; and she had friends who loved her as much as she loved them.

Three more hours until training. Liam had said they were going to start their foxtrot routine today and spend the rest of the week polishing it. Learning the routine would definitely take her mind off today. Even though he could lead her through it, she'd still have to remember all the sequences and count her way through until she was confident.

Somehow she managed to fill the time until she could head for Liam's studio. He made no comment when she walked in, so either he didn't know what today was or he'd decided to be kind and not mention it. And she managed to smile until he switched on the music and the first notes filled the air.

She recognised it instantly.

Oh, no. Of all the songs he could've picked, why did it have to be this one?

She steeled herself as the vocals began. It didn't matter. She could do this. *Think positive*, she told herself; at least she knew the song, so that was one less unfamiliar thing to deal with. And she forced herself to listen to Liam, let him talk her through the routine before they started dancing together.

Liam looked at Polly through narrowed eyes. She was crying. Silently, but she was still crying, the tears brimming over her lashes and rolling un-checked down her face.

What was going on? He wasn't asking her to do anything more difficult than she'd done in the last week.

'OK. Four basics, then two promenades,' he said. Once she'd started the routine, she'd realise it wasn't going to be problematic and everything would be fine. She'd stop crying.

He hoped.

To his relief, she didn't miss a single step.

'Corner,' he said, glancing swiftly at her. Then he realised that her tears hadn't stopped. At all. She was still silently weeping, the tears running unchecked down her cheeks.

This time, she stumbled. 'Sorry.' Her voice was quavery.

And then she pulled her hands away from the ball-room hold so she could cover her face with them. Her shoulders were shaking, and Liam could hear that she was trying to gulp back the sobs.

He couldn't ignore this any more and try to make her dance on, regardless. Even though he wanted to back away, because seeing such raw, painful emo-tion bursting through someone's defences made him feel incredibly uncomfortable.

The Polly he'd come to know wasn't a crier. What-ever had upset her had to be something major. She needed a shoulder to cry on—and right now he was the only person who could fill that role, whether he liked it or not. He had to make the effort.

'Polly,' he said softly.

She gulped. 'Sorry, I forgot where I was. What's the next step?'

'Polly, you can't cry and dance.'

'I'm not crying. I'm fine.'

He reached out and brushed a tear away with the pad of his thumb. 'No, you're not. And I'm being a selfish jerk, trying to pretend this'll all go away if I ignore it.' He bit back a sigh. 'What's wrong?'

How could she tell him? Once Liam knew about Harry, she knew he'd treat her differently and she couldn't bear that. She didn't want his pity.

She shook her head, unable to put it into words.

'We need a break. Go and put the kettle on,' he said.

She knew Liam was giving her some space, and she was glad of the chance to scrub her face with a tissue and breathe hard enough to stop the tears.

When the kettle was just about to boil, he walked into the kitchen and handed her a bar of chocolate.

'Where did you get this?' she asked.

'Amanda's secret stash. I'll replace it before she gets in on Monday, but right now I think your need is greater.'

His kindness made her want to cry all over again. She knew her tears had made him uncomfortable.

The awkwardness had been written all over this face. She'd expected him to be caustic about her inability to concentrate—and now he'd done this. Camera Liam. Or was this Real Liam?

'Thank you.' She bit into the confectionery. The rush from the sugar and the cocoa felt good.

He took over making the coffee. 'Better?' he asked, handing her a mug of coffee.

'Yes,' she lied.

'So are you going to tell me?'

She dragged into a breath. 'I know you've been working really hard on the choreography, and I'm being ungrateful, but I…' She shook her head. 'I'm sorry. I just can't dance to that song.'

'It brings back bad memories for you?' he guessed.

'Not bad memories, exactly.' She grimaced. 'It's something that never happened.'

He frowned. 'I'm not with you.'

She lifted her chin. 'If I tell you, I don't want you to treat me any differently. No pity, no condescension, no cotton wool. OK?'

Liam knew exactly where she was coming from. After the accident, pity was all he'd faced. He'd been at screaming point. And then, when Bianca left him, there had been more and more of the same. People seemed to stop seeing him for himself; it was as if he'd had the word 'victim' tattooed across his forehead.

'OK. It's a deal,' he promised, knowing already what she was going to tell him. That she'd been dumped. And somehow he'd have to find some words to bolster her.

'Today's my wedding day.'

*Her wedding day?* Now that he hadn't expected. The gossip rag hadn't said that her engagement had ended only a few days before she was supposed to get married—just that Harry had broken up with her and gone off with someone else.

Liam stared at her in shock. He'd had no idea that she'd been coping with this much of a mess.

'Well, it *was* going to be my wedding day,' she amended, 'until last week.'

Liam still didn't have a clue what to say. And that only added to the guilt he felt about not comforting her earlier.

'And this—' she lifted her chin and treated him to her brightest smile, which he knew now was a sure sign that her heart was breaking '—this was going to be the song for the first dance.'

'I'm sorry. If I'd known, I would've picked something different.'

'I should've said something. Except it wasn't on the list of songs you sent me, so I assumed it wasn't one you were thinking about using.' She lifted one shoulder. 'I didn't want to tell you before because—well, I didn't want you to start pitying me. I don't want to be this pathetic, needy creature.'

'I know where you're coming from. And you're not pathetic.' Needy, yes. But who was he to judge? 'I saw the stuff in the paper. But I had no idea he'd called it off this close to the wedding. That's rough on you.'

'It could have been worse. He could have just not turned up at the church today. At least he told me himself and he didn't leave it up to his best man or what have you to do the deed.'

Though Harry hadn't spared her those terrible photographs in the gossip rags, Liam thought. The photographs of Polly with empty eyes, looking as if her world had ended.

'Or, worse still, he could have married me today and then realised it was a mistake, so we would've had a legal mess to sort out as well as an emotional one.'

Yeah. Liam knew all about that one. Been there, done that, got the rights to the merchandising.

And she must really, really love the guy if she could come up with all these excuses for his behaviour when he'd clearly hurt her so badly.

'There's an awful lot to sort out if you cancel something at the last minute,' Liam said. 'I hope he was the one who had to ring up and cancel everything.'

She shook her head. 'No, that was my job.'

Liam whistled. The guy had called it off, but he'd

still made Polly pick up all the pieces? 'What a self-ish…' The curse slipped out before he could stop it.

'It's not like that. Harry's a creative.'

'He's a *what*?' This was like no excuse Liam had ever heard before.

'He produces TV programmes. He's great at putting things together and seeing where the real story is behind things, but he's really not very good at organising things outside a TV studio. So if I sort it out, at least I know it's done and nothing's been forgotten.' She shrugged. 'Anyway, I was the one who organised the wedding, so I had all the contacts. It was much easier for me to be the one to cancel things.'

She was underplaying it, Liam knew. Because Harry had left her to make all the explanations as well as cancel all the arrangements.

'It's still unfair that he left it to you to sort everything out. And to tell everyone.'

'If I'd left it to him, Liam, he wouldn't have done it. Someone else would've had to do it,' she said quietly.

The penny dropped: Harry would've talked his new girl into sorting things out for him. Cancelling the wedding to her predecessor. Liam winced. 'Oh, Pol.'

'No pity. You promised,' she reminded him.

'No. But I don't get why he'd do that to you.'

She sighed. 'He couldn't help falling in love with

someone else. He hated himself for breaking up with me. But he couldn't live a lie. We would both have ended up being miserable.'

'Are you telling me you're still friends?' Liam couldn't keep the note of disbelief from his voice.

'Not right now, no. But one day, we will be. We were friends before we got engaged. Good friends. We *liked* each other.' She swallowed hard. 'I thought that would make the difference and would mean that our marriage would last, because we had more than just some kind of fleeting passion. Except...' She shrugged. 'That wasn't what he wanted in the end. He wanted the kaboom.'

He didn't have a clue what she was talking about. 'What's the kaboom?'

'Harry says it's like fireworks going off in your head when you meet the right one.'

'Hmm.' Liam couldn't remember now if he'd had fireworks in his head with Bianca. Everything that came afterwards had kind of wiped that out. 'So is that why you're not working on *Monday Mash-up* any more?'

She nodded. 'I resigned. I couldn't face it.'

'Seeing him every day, you mean?'

'No.' She coughed. 'Seeing the producer's new assistant.'

Liam made the connection instantly. 'Surely she should've been the one to go, not you?'

'It was easier for everyone this way. It was my choice to leave.'

'Constructive dismissal, my brother would say—he's a lawyer,' Liam added. He remembered she'd said something about a new flat. Clearly she'd been living with Harry, before. 'So you were forced out of your engagement, your home and your job, all at the same time.' Pretty much how he'd been. Except he'd lost his marriage, his flat and his career because of a road accident, not someone else's selfishness.

She shrugged. 'It's character-building. Don't they say what doesn't kill you makes you stronger?'

Yeah. He knew all about that.

She pinned a huge smile to her face. 'Anyway, I'm fine now. Thanks for the break. And for—well, for being kind. I didn't expect that.'

'I'm not a total jerk, Polly.'

'I didn't mean that. But—well, you keep yourself separate.'

'Yes.' Because it was safe.

And he knew she was letting him off explaining when she said brightly, 'Let's go back and practise those steps.'

'Pol—'

'No pity, remember?' she cut in.

'No pity,' Liam agreed. 'I know what it feels like when you can see it in people's eyes when they look at you, and you know they're desperately glad it's not them in your shoes.' He held her gaze. 'I assume you know about my accident.'

'That you were badly injured and you recovered, yes. But it's none of my business.' She bit her lip. 'Except I worry that I'm going to trip and it'll jar your back and do some damage.'

He resisted the urge to touch her cheek to comfort. Just. Which in itself was worrying. He hadn't wanted contact like this for more than a year, not since Bianca. Why now? Why Polly? 'Thank you for thinking of me, but you really don't have to worry. You're not going to hurt my back, even if you do trip over me.'

'I take it that's how you know about pity?'

'That, and when Bianca dumped me for her new dancing partner. We didn't know if I'd recover enough to dance again at all, let alone in world-class competitions, and it would have been stupid to let the accident wipe out her career as well as mine. I was happy for her to dance with someone else. It made sense.' He gave an awkward shrug. 'I just wasn't expecting her to fall in love with the guy. Especially so fast. And then she left me for him.' And crushed what was left of his heart. Something he kept a thick barrier round now.

Except Polly's tears had unexpectedly put a crack in that barrier. He needed to put that right, the second she left his studio. But her eyes were still wet and he couldn't bring himself to suggest that she went home. He'd been that lonely and miserable, once. And, even though his head told him not to get involved, this was just too much for him to resist.

Polly hadn't expected Liam to open up to her like this; but she guessed this was his way of telling her that he understood exactly how she was feeling right now. 'You've already been here.'

'It's not the best feeling in the world.'

'But moping about it doesn't make it better.' She'd been there before. Crying didn't help.

'I'll tell you what does make it better,' he said.

'What?'

'As they said in the old Fred Astaire movie, let's face the music and dance. We'll forget my routine for now—I'll work up another one with a different song and we'll do that tomorrow.'

She grimaced. 'I feel guilty that you've wasted all that work.'

'I'll use it somewhere else. Anyway, I like choreographing.' He gave her another of those rare smiles, and it made her feel warm inside. As if the sun had just come out. Which was ridiculous—they were indoors and it was evening. And they barely knew each other. And today she'd been supposed to be getting married to someone else. This was all so wrong.

'Trust me, it gets easier with time,' he said. 'Like dancing, you just have to work at it a bit.'

To Polly's surprise, she really did feel better when

they'd spent the next hour dancing, practising the steps he'd taught her during the week; he kept to up-beat, happy music, and she loved it when they did the whirling turns all the way down one side of the room and then the other. She could imagine how this would feel in a posh frock, with the skirt spinning out as they danced. Glitzy, ritzy, shiny and happy. Like a princess in her perfect world.

'Thanks—you're right, dancing does help to make it better,' she said when the last song had ended. She went to change her shoes. 'I'd better get out of your hair now and let you have at least some of your Saturday evening.'

Which was his cue to let her go. Except he wasn't quite ready to do that. After what she'd just told him, he couldn't help feeling protective towards her. Wanting to look after her a little bit. Which was dangerous for his peace of mind; if he had any sense, he'd just make some anodyne remark and let her go.

But his mouth had other ideas. 'I wasn't doing anything in particular, tonight.' He paused. 'I assume you're going back to an empty flat?'

She nodded. 'I spent today scrubbing it. Not that I've lived there long enough to make much mess, and Fliss—my best friend—helped me move my stuff and clean it, the day I got the flat.' She shrugged. 'Still. It's a new start. And I have a new job to keep me busy—at least, for as long as I can try not to get us chucked out of the competition.'

'No chance. We're in this all the way to the final.'

'You betcha.' Though her words sounded hollow.

'Did you eat before you came here?'

She wrinkled her nose. 'I wasn't hungry.'

He frowned. 'Polly, you have to eat.'

'I know. I'm not going to starve myself to make other people feel guilty. That's not who I am.' She shrugged. 'I'm just not feeling that hungry today.'

'There are two sorts of people: those whose appetite goes when they're stressed, and those who eat everything in sight. I have to admit, I stuffed my face with cake when Bianca left.' He gave her a rueful look. 'I put on ten pounds in a month.'

She winced. 'Ouch.'

'The actual ouch bit was having to work it all off again with muscles that I hadn't been able to use for months—believe me, they really didn't want to play ball.'

'It must've been really hard for you.'

'About the same as it is for you, right now,' he said. 'I'd lost my career, I'd lost my marriage—and, yes, I lost my home as well, because obviously we had to split our assets in the divorce and it was easiest to sell the flat. Right at that point, I felt that there was nothing left. But I learned something, Polly. I *did* have something left.' He paused. 'I still had me. The one person in my life I can rely on.'

\* \* \*

He'd been exactly where she was. Except in an even worse place, really, because he'd thought he'd never be able to do what he loved again. She could still do what she loved—well, she could when she found another job. Or maybe she could come up with a concept for a new show and pitch it to one of Harry's competitors.

And Liam was right. She still had herself. She could definitely rely on herself. Though she had good friends she could rely on, too. Had it not been like that for him? On impulse, Polly reached out and squeezed his hand. 'Thank you, Liam.'

He returned the pressure, making little shivers run up her spine. 'No worries. Been there, done that, come out the other side.'

'And so will I.'

'Good.' He paused. 'Do you like Chinese food?'

'Yes.'

'I was planning on a takeaway dinner tonight. You could join me, if you like,' he suggested. 'There's not far to go, either—my flat's on the top floor of the building.'

Go home alone to an empty flat. Or take a risk. Get to know Liam a little better.

'Just so you know,' he said softly, 'I'm not coming on to you.'

Which was a relief. And, weirdly, it was a disappointment, too. Which again felt wrong. She hadn't expected Liam to stir these kinds of emotions in her. Why couldn't life be simple?

She pulled herself together. 'And it'll be OK with your, um, partner if I join you?'

'Just me. I've been single since Bianca left, and that's the way I'm keeping it. I'm concentrating on getting my career back,' Liam said. 'And I guess it's the same for you, after Harry. So we're colleagues.' He paused. 'We could be friends. Come and have some Chinese food with me.'

Put like that, how could she refuse? 'Thanks. I'd like that. Provided we go halves on the bill.' She wasn't giving up her independence.

'Deal,' he said.

And Polly knew that tonight wasn't going to be the second most miserable night of her life, after all.

# CHAPTER FIVE

LIAM'S flat turned out to be neat and very tidy, much like his office and his dance studio. Polly followed him into the kitchen, where he took a takeaway menu out of a drawer and waved it at her. 'Is there anything in particular you like or loathe?' he asked.

'I like most things, except hot prawns,' she said.

'Noted.' He rang the Chinese takeaway and ordered a variety of dishes. 'They should be here in about half an hour.' He rummaged in the fridge. 'White wine OK?'

'Yes, thanks.'

He poured two glasses, handed one to her, and ushered her into the living room. It was uncompromisingly masculine, with no cushions and no ornaments of any kind: just a leather sofa, one small bookcase, a television and what looked like state-of-the-art audio-visual equipment. Or maybe, like her, he hadn't moved in that long ago and hadn't had time to unpack most of his stuff.

'How long have you lived here?' she asked.

'About a year.'

Her thoughts must have shown on her face, because he said, 'I'm not keen on clutter and dusting. I'd rather have everything put away.'

'I kind of expected to see a cupboard full of trophies,' she said. 'I know you've won loads of competitions.'

He shrugged. 'Jointly, so Bianca took a lot of them. The rest are packed away.'

Because they were too painful to look at, she guessed. Bringing back memories of who he'd been and who he couldn't be again.

There were no photographs on the mantelpiece, either—so was he, like her, not very close to his family? Yet he'd mentioned a brother who was a lawyer.

It didn't feel polite to ask. And it was none of her business anyway. He'd tell her if he wanted her to know.

She sat awkwardly on the sofa, not knowing what to say. This felt almost like a first date—the getting-to-know-you, putting-your-foot-in-it stage. And it really wasn't how she'd been expecting to spend this evening. Right up until ten days ago, she'd been expecting to spend it dancing and laughing and enjoying herself with people she loved—and instead she was sitting here in silence with a near-stranger who'd had his life knocked off course the same way that she had. A stranger who looked absolutely gorgeous and could take her breath away with his rare smiles—and who could clam up and stick a wall round himself quicker than anyone she'd ever met.

As if he was thinking along similar lines, he blew out a breath. 'Sorry. My social skills are a bit rusty.'

'It's OK.' She gave him a bright smile.

'So you live up to your name. Polly Anna. Seeing all the positive things.'

'Yes.' It was the one thing her parents had done right: naming her. 'It helps, finding something good in a tough situation.'

'Hence the smile.'

'Something like that.' She wasn't going to tell him that her counsellor had given her a version of the Chaplin song when she was fifteen and the lyrics had helped her put her world back together. 'Smile, and it makes things better.'

'Not always.'

'We'll have to agree to disagree on that one,' she said.

Finally, his intercom rang to let them know that their meal had arrived. Liam buzzed the delivery boy up, taking crockery and cutlery from cupboards and drawers while they waited, and then Polly helped him unpack the box at the kitchen table. Several times her fingers brushed against his and it sent an odd frisson down her spine.

'Help yourself,' he said when they'd opened the last carton.

Polly couldn't resist the dim sum.

'Good?' he asked.

'Try some.' Without thinking, she leaned across the table, offering him one of the tiny steamed dumplings on her fork.

Colour stained his cheeks and his eyes widened.

Oh, help. What on earth did she think she was doing? They were practically strangers, and she was treating him like a best friend-cum-hot date. Not good. 'Sorry,' she muttered. 'I, um, forgot where I was.' She snatched her fork back.

Liam couldn't remember the last time he'd shared a meal with someone in such an intimate way. And he was oh, so tempted to lean across the table and draw her hand up towards his mouth, so he could finish what she'd just started. Worse still, he could imagine himself feeding her a morsel. Breakfast. In bed. A new-season strawberry, still warm from the sun—making her reach up for it, then tasting the juice of the fruit on her lips.

Oh, help. He needed to get a grip. And somehow defuse the tension in the room; it felt as if all the air had been sucked out.

'Do you—?' she began, at the same time as he said, 'Have you—?'

'Sorry. You first,' she said.

'No, you're my guest.'

She shook her head. 'I can't remember what I was

going to say now. But thanks. For bailing me out and not making me feel even more of an idiot.'

'You're not an idiot. Most women would've screamed and wailed about it long before now.'

'I don't scream. Ever.' Polly had lived through too many fights and too much screaming. 'It doesn't change things.'

'"Full of sound and fury, signifying nothing,"' he quoted.

Polly felt her eyes widen. 'I didn't peg you as a culture vulture.'

'Not all dancers are vain airheads,' he pointed out.

'Says the man who works in a room covered with mirrors.' For a moment, she thought she'd gone too far. And then he laughed. She hadn't heard him laugh before, and it was a revelation. A rich, amused chuckle that made her toes curl with pleasure. And she was shockingly aware of how attractive Liam was. The man he could be, when he didn't keep himself locked up. Though, given what he'd told her about Bianca, she could understand why he kept himself separate. She was planning to do that herself where her love life was concerned.

Liam wouldn't let her wash up, afterwards, but made them both a mug of coffee while she sorted out her half of the bill. Then her phone beeped, signalling a text message.

'Are you going to answer that?' Liam asked.

She wrinkled her nose. 'I don't want to be rude.'

'It might be important.'

'It's probably just Fliss—my best friend—checking that I'm OK.' She grabbed her phone from her handbag, checked the screen and typed in a rapid answer to reassure Fliss. 'Sorry about that. She worries about me. So do the *Monday Mash-up* boys.' She swallowed hard. She was *not* going to cry all over him again. 'I guess Danny, Charlie and Mike are like the brothers I don't have.'

'So that's why your phone beeps for ages when you switch it back on after a training session? They're all checking you're OK?'

She nodded. 'Sorry. It must be annoying for you.'

'No. It's good to have friends looking out for you.'

Something in his tone alerted her. 'Didn't your friends do that, after your accident?'

'Yes and no.' He grimaced. 'A lot of them were worried about seeing me. They thought it'd be like rubbing it in, because they could still dance and I couldn't.'

She frowned. 'I know I only met you a week ago, but that doesn't sound like the way you'd react.'

'It isn't. I guess they didn't know me as well as I thought they did. It was good just to talk about dancing—and, even if I couldn't dance again, I still intended to be involved in dance. Choreography.'

'Is that what you want to do after the competition—choreograph things?' she asked.

He nodded. 'I want to choreograph a musical for Broadway or the West End. I've done most of the routines for the professionals on *Ballroom Glitz*, this series.'

'So you need to win the competition, to get the producers to notice you.'

He shrugged. 'Being in the final would do.'

'No pressure, then,' she said wryly.

'What about you?' he asked.

'Hopefully, being on *Ballroom Glitz* will bring me to the attention of another producer and give me a chance to do something else in children's TV. Or maybe… It's probably a bit too ambitious, given that I'm not exactly an A-lister, but I've had enough experience now to know what works with kids. I might put together a proposal for a show and pitch it to the networks.'

'Another children's show?'

At her nod, he said, 'So you prefer working with kids rather than, say, acting onstage or on screen?'

'Absolutely. You get really spontaneous reactions from kids, much more than you do with adults, and it makes the live shows more interesting. You have to think on your feet.'

'Was the whole show live?' He grimaced. 'Sorry, that's rude. I ought to know that.'

She laughed. 'You're hardly our target audience. Most of the people who watch us are aged between nine and about fourteen.'

'And I don't have kids,' he said. 'Though Amanda says her kids love the show.'

'Thank you.' She remembered his question. 'About two-thirds of it's live; the rest is pre-recorded. We all have different slots. "Charlie's Charts" is where he goes through the new music releases that week, with video clips. "Mike's Movies" is—well, obvious.' She smiled. '"Danny's Dance" is where he teaches some of the kids in the studio a street-dance move, and then I have "Challenge Polly Anna". It started off as "Polly's Puzzles", where I'd give everyone a brain teaser to solve, but then one day one of the kids in the studio gave me a challenge in return, and it snowballed from there. So I've done everything from being able to eat a doughnut without licking my lips, through to juggling raw eggs.'

Liam raised an eyebrow. 'How many did you break?'

'Enough for a few omelettes,' she said with a grin. 'I practised with rubber eggs until I was nearly there.'

'You don't give up until you've done whatever it is, do you?'

'I try not to, though sometimes I haven't been able to beat the challenge. I really couldn't get the hang of roller skating, so ice skating was a definite no-no.'

'Noted.' He looked thoughtful. 'You know, we could get juggling into a routine. A circus theme for the jive, maybe. I'll think about it.'

'I'm in your hands.' Then she realised how cheesy that sounded. 'Not that I was coming on to you,' she added swiftly.

'Of course not.'

Polly glanced at her watch, and was surprised by how late it was. 'I'd better go home.'

'I'll drive you.'

'No, it's fine. I can take the Tube, and I'm sure you have other things to do anyway.'

'I do have some paperwork to go through,' he admitted. 'But I don't want you walking anywhere. It's pouring with rain. I'll call you a cab—and don't argue. If you're sneezing your way through the routine next Saturday, you're not going to enjoy it, are you?'

And if she was distracted by fighting off some bug or other, she was more likely to go wrong following the steps of the routine. She wasn't naïve enough to think that his concern was all for her. 'I guess you have a point. Thank you.'

He rang the taxi company. When he put the phone down, he said, 'They'll be here in fifteen minutes.'

'Thank you.'

They looked at one another in silence for a moment and the atmosphere became charged. Liam thought of something quickly to say.

'So, our training tomorrow. Does the afternoon work for you? It'll give me a chance to sort out a new routine in the morning.'

'I'm sorry about that.' Deciding to be brave, she lifted her chin. 'Look, I can give your original routine a go.'

'To the song you planned as the first dance at your wedding reception?' He shook his head. 'I'm not going to put you through that. Anyway, as I said, I like choreographing. Is "Beyond the Sea" OK for you?' He hummed the first few bars of the old Bobby Darin song.

Recognising it, Polly remembered that they'd danced to it before. 'That's absolutely fine.'

'Good.'

Then the intercom buzzed. 'That's your taxi.'

'OK. I'll see you tomorrow afternoon.' She paused. 'And thank you for this evening.' For not letting her go home to a lonely, empty flat.

'No worries. I'll see you downstairs.'

'There's no need, really. I think I can just about manage a couple of flights of stairs.'

'You can manage anything you put your mind to. And that includes nailing our routine.'

Liam really intended just to shake her hand. In a brotherly way. Except he found himself dipping his head and kissing her on the cheek. Hesitant, a little awkward; but her skin was so soft around his lips, and he could smell that sweet, fresh, floral scent she wore. He couldn't resist the temptation to linger. And he only just managed to stop himself kissing a line from her cheek to the corner of her mouth—and then taking it further.

The kiss on the cheek was just like any of the team on *Monday Mash-up* would have done.

Except this didn't feel like a brotherly kiss. Where Liam's lips touched Polly's skin, they made every nerve-end tingle.

Though she was just being ridiculous, she told herself on the way home in the taxi. Nice Liam wasn't just for the cameras; she had a feeling that that was who he really was. Who he'd always been. But the accident and Bianca's betrayal had made him grow a shell to cover up that niceness. Being Mr Snippy meant that he didn't let people close to him—and that in turn meant he wouldn't get hurt.

The fact that he was starting to open up to her, be Nice Liam again... Well, if he wanted her to trust him, he had to trust her, too. Maybe he'd worked that out for himself.

And she was overanalysing things. Overreacting to a kiss that hadn't meant anything more than it would've done from Danny, Mike or Charlie. She was stupid to wish for more; or maybe she was just overemotional and mixed-up, given what today should've been.

She let herself into the flat. Although it was tiny, it felt *empty*.

'Polly Anna Adams, don't you dare be so wet,' she told herself.

And she wasn't going to let herself think about what Harry was doing tonight.

At all.


On Sunday, Polly arrived at Liam's studio in the afternoon, as they'd arranged.

Would he mention the kiss? she wondered. Would it have changed things between them? Would he throw up a huge brick wall between them?

His expression was unreadable. She really wasn't sure which way this was going to go. His eyes narrowed slightly, as if he'd noticed the shadows beneath her eyes; but then he seemed to switch into professional mode.

'Ready for the routine?' he asked.

'Sure,' she said, glad to follow his lead. Glad that he wasn't going to overanalyse that kiss on her cheek—she'd already done that more than enough.

The music was upbeat, lively and fun. He broke the routine down into segments for her and talked her through the steps.

'I can't believe you've put this routine together so quickly.'

He shrugged off the compliment, though a glitter in those gorgeous navy blue eyes told her that he was pleased. 'I told you I liked choreographing.'

The training session went incredibly quickly; at

the end, Liam said, 'I've been thinking. You really ought to go to the wardrobe department tomorrow afternoon to sort out your dress for Saturday. And it might be useful to practise the last few days of the routine in a skirt, so wearing the costume doesn't throw you on the night.'

Polly bit her lip. The wardrobe department. They'd styled her as Audrey Hepburn, last time; hopefully this time they'd give her a pair of long gloves again, or if not then a dress with long sleeves. Or maybe she could tell them she was superstitious and she'd get stage fright with short sleeves...

Though she knew that Liam wouldn't buy that. Eventually, he'd ask why she always covered her wrists. But she couldn't face telling him the shameful truth.

She cleared her throat. 'Were you planning to go with me?'

'I'm teaching the cast a new routine tomorrow. If you're desperate for a second opinion, I can probably spare you five minutes. But the show's been running for six years, now, and Rhoda in the wardrobe department's very experienced. You'll be fine.'

'So does she choose the dress for me?'

'She'll probably offer you a selection,' Liam explained. 'She knows you're dancing the foxtrot, so she'll find you some costumes that suit the dance—but it's your choice within that selection. I'll be in a black tailcoat with a white shirt and a white tie, so you won't clash with me, whatever colour you choose.'

'Any colour I like?' she tested.

He wrinkled his nose. 'Maybe not *quite* as bright as the stuff you used to wear on *Monday Mash-up*.'

She laughed. 'Very tactful. OK. Noted. Something classy. Anything else I need to look for?'

'Keep the hem of your dress just above your ankle, so your heel won't catch in the material, and pick shoes with a similar heel height to the ones you've been dancing in. And you'll need to dance in them for the rest of the week, so you get used to the weight and the feel of them.'

'OK.' She summoned up a smile. 'See you tomorrow.'

Monday's training session went well, but Polly's confidence had evaporated by the time she got to the wardrobe department. Thankfully one of the dresses Rhoda had selected for her had long sleeves; it was the right length, too. Sea green and floaty, with silver shoes.

Looking at herself in the mirror, Polly thought, *Nobody at* Monday Mash-up *would recognise me.* She wasn't sure she recognised herself. But that was a good thing—wasn't it?

'So what's your dress like?' Liam asked Polly, the next morning.

'Green.'

He raised an eyebrow

'What's the problem?' she asked.

'You're not superstitious, then?'

She rolled her eyes. 'Don't tell me you are.'

'No.' But he didn't sound too sure.

'It's all rubbish about green being an unlucky colour. And yellow. I used to wear lime green all the time on *Monday Mash-up*.'

'Lime green,' he said, sounding thoughtful. 'Is that what you chose?'

Unable to resist teasing him, she pointed out, 'You said I wouldn't clash with you, whatever I chose.'

'Lime green. Okay-y-y,' he said. 'Tomorrow, you need to wear a skirt to training. Did you bring your shoes?'

'I forgot,' she admitted. 'I'll bring them tomorrow.'

'And they match your dress?'

'They're silver,' she said. Which would tell him nothing about the colour of her dress. 'You'll see the dress on Saturday.'

But she duly wore a skirt and the silver shoes on Wednesday. They polished the routine on Thursday and Friday, pausing only to do a quick video of their training progress for the *Step by Step* programme. By the end of the last training session, Polly was totally sick of 'Beyond the Sea' and swore privately that she'd never, ever listen to the song again after the show on Saturday.

'Do something that helps you relax, tonight,' Liam said as she was about to leave the studio. 'Read a good book or curl up on the sofa with a film.'

She scoffed. 'I'm surprised you're not telling me to go on a five-mile run.'

'No, that's what *I'd* do to relax.'

'So are we training tomorrow morning?'

'No, because we have a dress rehearsal in the afternoon. I don't want to overdo things. See you tomorrow on the set.'

On Saturday afternoon, Polly turned up at the TV studios for the dress rehearsal, and changed into her dress. She knew that Liam would be in a tailcoat, but even so she wasn't prepared for how gorgeous he looked.

And getting the shivers when she saw him was utterly ridiculous. He'd made it very clear that he wasn't interested in her beyond teaching her to dance for the competition. He wasn't interested in a relationship, full stop. He was focused on getting his career back. And she was behaving like a newly hatched chick, trying to bond with the first person she saw.

Be professional, she told herself, and held her head high as she walked over to him.

Last time, the wardrobe department had styled Polly as Audrey Hepburn. Today, she took his breath away. The dress was floaty and elegant, and, although she looked slightly nervous, she looked beautiful. Like Sleeping Beauty when the prince's kiss had first woken her.

And Liam was shocked to find himself wondering what it would be like to kiss her. Properly this time...

But this wasn't part of the deal. It wasn't what either of them needed right now. And he didn't have a clue what to say to her. He had a nasty feeling that if he opened his mouth, the wrong words would come out. Words that could embarrass both of them. They couldn't afford to cross that line.

He managed to get his head back in control—just—by the time Polly joined him. Teasing. That was the way to go. She'd teased him about the colour of her dress. He could tease her. Play the boy next door. And it might stop him wanting much, much more.

'Lime green, indeed,' he said with a grin.

Except then he ruined it by being unable to resist running one finger down her long sleeve.

Polly went absolutely still. This was crazy. Why was her skin tingling? He hadn't even touched her—just the material of her dress.

Except her imagination was running overdrive on what it would feel like if he touched her skin. And that scared her. Why was she reacting this way to him? There was no point in starting something that just couldn't have a future. She didn't want a fling. She didn't think he did, either. Neither of them needed this kind of complication.

*Get a* grip, she told herself.

'This is sea green,' he said.

'Because of the song. It kind of went together for me.' That, and the fact that it had long sleeves.

'Good choice. It's lovely.'

But she had the distinct feeling that he was holding something back. 'You're not really superstitious, are you?'

'No. Though I don't go out of my way to walk under ladders, either.'

Perhaps Bianca had always worn green. Polly made a mental note to check out a few videos on the Internet, to make sure she didn't pick anything in the future that might remind Liam of his ex-wife.

The rehearsal went well, but Polly's nerves kicked in the second that the first couple took to the floor.

Liam laced his fingers through hers, giving them a reassuring squeeze. And how pathetic was she, wanting him to hold her hand?

'Remember, there are no eliminations in the first week,' he told her, 'just the critique from the judges—and they're all new judges this year.'

'Have you worked with any of them before?'

'Tiki, the choreographer, yes.' He grimaced. 'She always picks holes in people, so ignore whatever she says. I guess they've set her up as Miss Nasty; and

Mr Nice will be Robbie, the soap actor who won the competition last year. He'll be sweet and supportive to everyone because he'll remember what it feels like, being in your shoes. The one you need to pay attention to is Scott, the dancer—he'll give you the constructive comments, the stuff that will help you learn and improve.'

'Got it,' Polly said.

'Whatever happens tonight, it really doesn't matter. You can fall flat on your face, and it'll be just fine,' Liam reassured her.

It hadn't been fine in her dreams last night. She'd fallen flat on her face and they'd changed the rules of the show—they'd kicked her out in the very first week. Not that she'd dare confide that to him. It would send him straight into Mr Snippy mode.

Polly's nerves grew worse with every couple that went out from the Green Room to the dance floor. She knew the scheduling had been done fairly—the names had been picked out of a hat in front of all of them after the dress rehearsal. But she really, really wished that they'd been first. She wanted to get it over with. Being last was just the pits.

Finally Millie, the host, looking very glam in a little black dress and the highest heels Polly had ever seen, announced them: 'Dancing the foxtrot to "Beyond the Sea", it's Polly Anna Adams and Liam Flynn!'

Polly felt sick. She was used to having an attack

of nerves before going on the live set of *Monday Mash-up*, and in the past had always welcomed them because she thought they kept her sharp and helped her try her hardest to put a good show together. But this was nothing like she'd experienced before. She could barely move her feet.

The audience applauded as they walked onto the dance floor.

'Relax,' Liam said softly. 'Pretend we're in my studio and it's Amanda clapping us.'

And then the first notes of 'Beyond the Sea' floated into the air.

Oh, help. She'd forgotten every step he'd taught her. She'd forgotten which was her right and which was her left. And were her hands in the right place?

Then Liam moved, leading her round the dance floor. Making her feel lighter than air; yet, at the same time, she felt like a sack of potatoes. She was making a mess of this and showing him up, after all the hard work he'd put into teaching her. Any West End producers watching this would scrub his name straight off their lists. She'd let him down, and she was so cross with herself for it.

The song lasted for the longest three minutes of Polly's life.

And then finally it was over. She gave the audience a megawatt smile that she definitely didn't feel, and to her shock Liam stood back and directed the audience's applause to her, clapping along with them.

Why was he applauding her when she'd been so hopeless?

He slid one arm round her shoulders and walked with her over to the judges' table.

Tiki shook her head and compressed her lips. 'Polly Anna, your hands weren't quite right, your movements were too jerky, and you don't hold yourself straight enough.'

The audience booed, and Liam tightened his arm round her shoulders.

'And the routine was too simple.' She flapped a dismissive hand. 'Or maybe you couldn't cope with anything more.'

'May I say something, please?' Liam asked before Millie went to the next judge. At her nod, he continued, 'Polly's a total novice and she's worked incredibly hard the last couple of weeks. I think that deserves some recognition. I'm sorry you don't like the choreography—but that's my fault, not Polly's, so don't blame her for that.'

The audience clapped wildly; Tiki said nothing but scowled at Liam.

Hastily, Millie moved on to the next judge.

'Polly, Polly, Polly.' Robbie smiled at her. 'You and me, we both know what it's like being on set in front of a camera and doing bits of live shows. But *Ballroom Glitz* is different. You're in the spotlight, being watched by millions. It's *scary*. And you smiled all the way through it, so well done to you, girl.' The audience clapped loudly. 'I'm looking forward to seeing you shine next week.'

'Scott,' Millie said.

'You've made a good start. You can build on that and work on the polish. Your posture needs to be stronger and you need to be less worried about where you put your feet, but that'll come with practice. I'm looking forward to watching your confidence grow.' He smiled. 'Well done.'

'Remember what I said. Tiki's paid to be mean, Robbie's paid to be a sweetheart, and Scott's the serious one. He gave you some praise as well as saying what you need to work on,' Liam said as he led Polly off the dance floor and back to the Green Room.

They'd just sat down when the judges' scores were announced.

They'd been the last couple on; to Polly's shame, they were also the last on the leader board. By a very long way. As she'd expected, Lina the pop singer was top of the leader board, followed surprisingly by Bryan the TV gardener. But the gap between their scores and hers was huge.

'Sorry, Liam. I let you down.' That, or she shouldn't have worn an unlucky colour. If this happened next week, it would all be over. And right now she wasn't sure she'd manage to dance any better next week. She'd done her best and it wasn't good enough.

'You didn't let me down. Stop worrying.'

'Tiki didn't like us.'

'She didn't like anyone.' He spread his hands. 'Even if she gives someone a ten, she'll still find something to criticise.'

'We came last.'

'Which means the only way is up.'

Ha. That should be her line. But her confidence, already shaky thanks to Harry and Grace, had gone through the floor.

So Polly did what she always did. Faked it with a broad smile. 'Yeah. See you tomorrow for training.'

'Not so fast.' He laid a restraining hand on her arm. 'You're not going home to brood in an empty flat.'

'Of course I'm not.'

He rolled his eyes. 'Polly, I saw you smile like that last Saturday night.'

She flinched. How could he be mean enough to bring that up?

'I know you're going to brood,' he said, his voice a little gentler. 'So we're going for a drink.'

'Why?'

'To celebrate.'

'Celebrate? We came *last*,' she repeated. 'That's hardly a cause for celebration.'

'We have a baseline position,' he corrected. 'Something we can work with. Get changed. I'll see you in ten minutes.'

Polly couldn't think of any arguments, and she

still couldn't by the time she'd changed and met Liam in the corridor. Or when he took her to a small club where a band was playing soft jazz-blues numbers. She was still angry with herself for letting him down—for letting herself down, too—but the music did a lot to soothe her soul. As did the two glasses of white wine he persuaded her to drink.

And then the band played the opening of 'Beyond the Sea'.

'They're playing our tune.' Liam gestured to the dance floor. 'Shall we?'

Dance, to the song she'd messed up? 'I'm not dressed for dancing,' she said. Her black trousers and black long-sleeved top were hardly dressy enough to go out for a drink, let alone anything else.

'It doesn't matter. Nobody's watching.'

He was right. It didn't matter, not like tonight's performance. So she let him lead her onto the dance floor. Stood in hold with him. Let him guide her round the tiny dance floor. Sang along to the words.

And he was smiling as they danced. Not a mocking smile—a real, genuine smile. As if he were enjoying her company. Enjoying the dance.

So was she.

Because here, away from the spotlights and the judges, it worked. The floating feeling was back. She wasn't scared that she'd miss a step, because it really didn't matter if she did. This wasn't for show. It was just for them. For fun.

There were other couples on the dance floor, but she barely noticed them. All she could focus on was Liam. She was shockingly aware of how close he was to her and how his legs slid between hers and hers slid between his as they turned. He was holding her so close that she could actually feel the heat of his body. And, at the end of the dance, when he spun her out in a twirl and then back into his arms, holding her closer still, her heart skipped a beat.

This was nothing like their dance earlier tonight. This was intense, sharp, sexy—and the adrenalin pumping through her blood wasn't from nerves, as it had been earlier. This was fuelled by something else. Something she really hadn't expected.

She looked up at him, and could see the shock mirrored in his eyes.

So he felt it, too. And was just as shocked by it.

What next?

Would he want to see where this took them?

Would he dip his head to kiss her?

Did she want him to?

Time seemed to slow down. To stop.

But then the band segued into another song, one she and Liam had practised to. One she really liked; and as Liam brought her back into ballroom hold she found herself singing along to it. Even though the words were all about love and romance and dancing in the moonlight.

At the very end of the song, Liam lifted her up and

spun her round. And, as he set her down again, he held her close enough that she slid down his body. Her knees went weak, and if he hadn't been holding her tightly she would've fallen. For a moment his gaze held hers, dark and intense. She could feel her lips parting, inviting him to kiss her.

This would be total, utter madness. She needed to call a halt to it right now.

'I need a drink,' she mumbled.

'Water. We need to rehydrate,' he said huskily.

The shock on his face was so clear that she knew he'd been just about to kiss her. And that those feelings were just as unlooked-for and confusing for him as they were for her.

Somehow they had to get past this. Focus on what they both wanted: a new contract to take their careers forward.

Separately.

Knowing she was being a coward, she made an excuse when he came back from the bar with their water. 'I didn't sleep well last night.' She yawned. 'I'd better go home now so I'm up in time for training tomorrow.'

Was that relief or disappointment in his eyes? She couldn't be sure. And she didn't dare ask. But he ordered a taxi for her and waited with her until it arrived.

If only things were different, she thought as the cabbie took her home. If only she and Liam had met some other time. But this fledgling thing between them didn't stand a chance. So she'd just have to be sensible. And back off.

# CHAPTER SIX

POLLY'S heart was thudding when she pressed the intercom to Liam's studio the next morning. She'd slept badly again, brooding over those near-kisses and the way he'd made her feel when he'd held her close.

Even though her head told her she'd done the right thing, that Liam was as much of an emotional mess as she was and they'd be crazy to act on the attraction between them, her heart was still asking, 'what if'?

What if she'd been braver?

What if she hadn't backed away?

What if he'd kissed her?

She shook herself. They had a job to do. This week, she couldn't afford to let him down. For both their sakes, she had to get it right.

Her heartbeat was still racing when she'd climbed the two flights of stairs to the studio. Physical exercise, she told herself, knowing that she was lying:

she was nervous. How was Liam going to react to her? Would he pretend that nothing had happened?

When she opened the door, he looked as nervous as she felt. Worrying that she'd push him past his limits? Or worrying that she was going to bail out on him and his career was going to come crashing down again?

'Hi,' she said.

'Did you sleep well?' he asked.

So that was how he was playing it. Being nice, rather than snippy—but putting up another barrier. A different one. A polite one.

Well, she could do that, too.

'Yes,' she fibbed. 'Did you?'

'Yes.'

She'd bet that was just as much of a fib as hers. 'What am I learning today?' she asked, giving him her brightest smile.

He didn't call her on it. And again she wasn't sure if that was disappointment or relief she glimpsed briefly in his eyes.

'The cha cha cha. This is the week you learn that dancing can be fun.' He handed her a mug of coffee. 'Sit down and drink this while I show you the basic step.'

Polly was happy to sit cross-legged on the floor and watch him while she sipped her coffee.

'Remember how I taught you to shift the weight in the balance step when we did the foxtrot? It's the same thing, just this time it's forward and back. Rock, rock.' He demonstrated. 'And then we do a quick side-close-side. One, two, one-and-two.'

Amazingly, his body seemed to just move from the hips; his upper body was perfectly straight and still. How did he do that? 'You have very good posture,' she said. 'Snake hips.' And then she blushed. Would he take it the wrong way? Would it make him think of last night, the way they'd been so close?

He stayed in teaching mode. 'The key to this dance is the hip action. You need to try to keep your legs straight.'

'And that's it for the basic step?'

'You do a set to one side, then a set back again—and, once you've got that going, you can add some bits onto it to make it interesting.'

Polly put her mug down carefully, relieved that she didn't spill coffee all over his expensive floor. 'So I guess it's my turn to do this now?'

'Yup. We're going to do this one side by side until you get the basic step—you can see what I'm doing in the mirror and you do exactly the same as I do,' Liam said. 'We're going to do it really slowly at first.'

He talked her through a set to the left and a set to the right, then gave her a thoughtful look. 'OK, but there's one thing I need to pick you up on. When you rock back, don't go back on your heel and lift your toes—the judges will mark you down for that. If it makes it a little easier for you, step it out, but just remember to keep your toes on the floor.'

'Right.'

'Let's keep going.' He continued talking her through the basic step, and gradually their movements sped up.

Then he took her hand and spun her round to face him. 'Well done. You've got the hang of the basic step. Now we'll do it face to face. The hold's a little bit looser than the foxtrot, but I'll explain why when I teach you some of the later steps.'

He wasn't holding her as close as he had for the foxtrot but, even so, Polly was very aware of the feel of his fingers against hers. Which was ridiculous. Her body shouldn't be so aware of him as this. And she shouldn't be wanting to press against him.

'Music, first.'

It was the best thing he could've done, because she relaxed when she recognised the old Abba song. 'I had no idea this was a cha cha cha. Though there's something different about it.'

'It's a remix. Especially for dance teachers.'

The beat was infectious, and to her surprise she found it much easier than the foxtrot. This didn't feel like hard work and counting. He was right: this was *fun*.

They took a break and went out for a late breakfast again.

'You're enjoying this one, aren't you?' Liam asked.

She nodded. 'It's a lot easier than the foxtrot.'

'You'll find that you'll really click with a couple of the dances, and you'll really not enjoy others.'

'Any clues as to which?'

He shook his head. 'It varies from person to person—and you might think before you start learning a dance that because you enjoy watching other people dancing it, you'll enjoy dancing it yourself, but then you'll discover it doesn't do anything for you.'

'Whereas something you might not bother watching turns out to be a lot more fun when you're actually doing it?' she guessed.

'Absolutely.'

Talking about dance had made him relax with her again. Wanting to keep that going, she asked, 'What's your favourite dance?'

'The rumba,' he said.

'Why?'

His eyes glittered. 'Because it's so sensual.'

Oh, the pictures *that* put in her head. She could feel the blush heating her entire body. If the rumba was more sensual than the way he'd danced with her last night, heaven help her. She'd go up in flames.

'And I have a soft spot for the cha cha cha. Come on, let's get back to it. I want to teach you how to do a New York. You tend to do it at the end of chassé— that's the "cha cha cha" step—and you'll know exactly when we're going to do this, because I'll let go of your right hand when we're moving to the right and place my left hand under yours.'

Back at the studio, he talked her through the move, doing everything at a slow walking pace.

'It's a bit like the promenade step,' she said, 'with our feet.'

'A bit,' he said, 'except you move your arm out to the side.' He talked her through the hand positions, then put the music on and practised the new step with her.

To her surprise, she found it easy. Compared to the effort she'd put into the foxtrot and the way she'd felt like a failure because she couldn't grasp it, this was like a dream. Something she hadn't believed possible.

'Ready to add another step?' he asked.

'Already?'

'Already,' he confirmed. 'This one's fun. It's called a spot turn, because you turn on the spot— and it's also why you need to keep your hand very loose in mine, otherwise you'll twist your arm.'

It took a little while for Polly to do it right but, when she finally managed to keep her feet still and spin round, it felt amazing. 'I can't believe it was so easy! Why was I having trouble with it?'

'Because you're still learning.' But he was smiling, and warmth spread through her. A genuine smile from Liam could send her temperature rocketing.

'It's really clicked, hasn't it?' he asked.

'How do you know?'

'Your eyes are shining.'

And how tempted Liam was to dip his head and kiss her. Not on the cheek, the way he did at the end of a lesson, but properly. The way he'd wanted to kiss her last night, when Polly had looked up at him with those huge eyes and parted lips. This was crazy. Neither of them was in the right place for a relationship, even for a fling. And he didn't want to take any risks, let someone that close to him again. This had to stop. Right now.

He held himself in check—just—and forced himself to concentrate on teaching her the steps instead of giving in to the temptation to pull her close and to hell with the dancing.

The rest of the lesson flew by. 'See you in the morning, then. Have a nice afternoon.' He waited until she'd gone before switching on the music system again and going through the latest routine he'd been working out for the professional dancers on the show.

But for once he found it hard to concentrate on the dancing. He kept thinking of Polly, the sweetness of her smile and the way her eyes had shone as she'd felt the magic of the dance. The way she'd been last night, when she'd finally relaxed with him and given herself over to the music. And he knew it could be oh, so good between them…

'You,' he told himself crossly, 'need your head examined. Focus.'

The next morning, Liam was teaching Polly a more complicated turn when Amanda came in to the studio. 'Liam, I know you never look at the show's message boards, and he's probably told you to ignore them, Polly, but I think you both really need to see this.'

'See what?' Polly asked.

Amanda produced a print-out with a flourish. 'This,' she said, 'is the poll—no pun intended, Pol—showing who's the most popular couple on the show. Have a look.'

The chart showed that Polly and Liam were top, by a long way.

'Wow. I never expected that—that's really…' Polly shook her head, unable to think of the right word. 'Well, it's humbling. Especially as we came last on the judges' scoresheets.'

'They really didn't like Tiki's reaction,' Amanda said. 'I've read all the threads. Everyone's backing you, Polly. Go for it.'

'And this is the dance to do it,' Liam said softly when Amanda left the studio again. 'Tomorrow, we'll start the routine. But I'm going to check the song with you first.'

He flicked a switch on his music system and an up-tempo song began; Polly recognised it as 'Sway'.

'I know that song. I've heard it on a film sound-track.'

'And you're OK with it?'

'I love it.' She listened for a bit, then started cha-cha-chaing to the music.

He raised an eyebrow. 'And you started dead in the right place. Good. I think this is definitely your dance, Pol.'

'Well, maestro—or whatever you're meant to call a dancer—let's go for it.'

Polly found herself humming the song all the way home. And even having to deal with more admin from the cancelled wedding didn't take the shine off her mood. She was still smiling the next morning, and this time she seemed to pick up the routine much more easily, not minding that Liam was bringing in more complicated underarm turns and mixing up dancing in hold with dancing side by side.

'You're doing well,' he said, and the unexpected praise made her feel hot all over.

'But?' She knew there would be a but.

He spread his hands. 'But I need to get you used to dancing the cha cha cha in something other than trousers. I'll come with you to the wardrobe depart-ment tomorrow, because they'll need to match my outfit to your dress.' He looked thoughtful. 'Something short and flirty, I think.'

That was bound to mean short sleeves. Panic flooded through her. 'Can't I have something floaty, like last week?'

'You can't do a Latin dance in a ballroom costume,' Liam said. 'And if Jane the comedienne can wear a short skirt, given that she's a fair bit, um, curvier than you, then you'll be fine.' He patted her shoulder. 'People will look at your feet and your smile, I promise.'

Obviously he thought she was panicking about her thighs. 'I'm not worried about my legs,' she said.

'Then what's wrong?'

She couldn't bring herself to tell him. The words stuck in her throat. The easy way out would be to show him the scars, but she just couldn't do that. 'I don't mind a short dress, but I'm used to long sleeves.'

'Not for a cha cha cha.'

'I'm superstitious,' she said.

His expression told her that, given she'd picked a green dress last time, he didn't believe a word of it. But, to her relief, he didn't push her on the subject.

On Wednesday morning, their practice went well and Polly's smile was genuine. But her smile faded when they went to the wardrobe department and she realised that none of the costumes on offer had long sleeves.

'I really need long sleeves,' she said to Rhoda, biting her lip. 'Please.'

'There aren't any—not with the cha cha cha dresses.'

Polly thought back to costumes she'd seen on the show in previous years. 'What about something with cuffs?'

'Ah—now, cuffs we can do,' Rhoda said.

The relief made Polly's knees go weak. Rhoda came back with a blue sequinned dress, the same dark blue as Liam's eyes; it had a fringed short skirt, a silver belt, and matching silver cuffs that Polly could see immediately would be deep enough to hide her scars. 'Those silver shoes you had for the foxtrot—they'll work for this, too,' Rhoda said.

'Thank you. That's absolutely brilliant.'

'My pleasure, love.' Though Rhoda looked concerned, and Polly had the nasty feeling she was going to be the centre of backstage...not gossip, exactly, but conversation.

She'd just have to hope that they'd find a more interesting topic.

Liam's outfit consisted of dark trousers, and a sheer dark blue shirt, shot through with silver and navy blue sequins.

'Flashy,' she teased.

But the shirt also brought out the beautiful colour

of his eyes; it really suited him. And she loved the swishy skirt of her dress.

'You know I'm going to ask—' Liam began when they'd left the studio.

'No.' In panic, she pressed the tip of her finger over his mouth. And then she wished she hadn't. His lips were warm. Soft. And the contact with her skin made her tingle all over.

'Please don't. It's something I don't want to talk about, OK?' Her voice was shaky, and not just because of dredging up her past. Touching Liam made her knees go weak.

'Is it something that's going to affect your dancing?'

'No.' Not unless she had to wear short sleeves. 'If you promise not to ask me, I'll cook you a pizza for dinner tonight.' The second she stopped speaking, she panicked again. Now he'd think she was asking him out on a date. And she wasn't—was she?

'That is, to say thanks for how much you've taught me this week,' she added swiftly.

'It's my job,' he reminded her.

'And good work gets a bonus. In this case, pizza.'

'Home made?' he asked.

'Well—no. But I make a mean brownie.'

'Cake.' His eyes glittered. 'Done. What time?'

'Seven?'

'Great. See you then.'

\* \* \*

Liam rang the doorbell at seven precisely; a few seconds later, Polly opened the door and her eyes widened as he handed her a bunch of bright pink gerbera.

'How lovely.' She beamed at him. 'Though you didn't have to do that.'

'Hostess gift,' he said. Just in case she thought there were strings attached.

'Thank you. Come in, and I'll put these in water.'

She rummaged through a cupboard in her kitchen. 'No vase. Stupid. I'll get one tomorrow.' She found a measuring jug, filled it with water and put the flowers in it.

Her smile had turned super-bright again, and guilt flooded through him. 'Sorry. I wouldn't have brought them if I'd known they'd upset you.'

'No, I love them. But they're the first flowers since…' Her voice tailed off.

He filled in the gap. Since her wedding-that-wasn't. 'I used to buy flowers for Bianca every Friday,' he said, and could've kicked himself. Why was he telling her that and making it worse?

'Harry wasn't one for flowers. I used to buy them for myself. Ones like this, that make everything look bright and happy. I must've left my vases at his place. Not that I want them back now.' She flapped a dismissive hand. 'I knew you'd be dead on time. The pizza will be here in ten minutes. Let me get you a drink. Wine?'

He handed her a bottle. 'My contribution. It should still be chilled.'

'Thank you.' She poured them both a glass. 'Do you want the grand tour? It'll take all of two minutes.'

She was talking way too much and way too fast, Liam thought. Nervous. Yeah. So was he. Which he really hadn't expected, because he was fine when he was teaching her. But being here, in her space—that shifted the balance. Changed things. 'The grand tour will be great.'

'Obviously this is the kitchen,' she said. 'Bathroom. My room.' He noticed that she kept that particular door closed. 'Living room.'

There were photographs and knick-knacks on every windowsill and shelf, along with plenty of books and films. Too busy for his taste, though it was spotlessly clean.

She'd clearly noticed him scanning the room. 'You think it's cluttered, don't you?'

'I'd put everything in cupboards,' he admitted. 'But each to their own.'

He followed her back to the kitchen, and looked at the photographs on her fridge. 'I assume these are the *Monday Mash-up* boys?'

'Yes. And this is Fliss, my very best friend, and Shelley and Carrie. They're the chick-flick chicks— their husbands all hate the kind of girly films we love, so we go without them and eat a ton of ice cream afterwards.'

There were plenty of photos of her with friends, he noticed, but not with anyone who looked enough like her to be a sibling or cousin, and none of her with anyone older. She hadn't mentioned her family at all.

And there was the fact that she insisted on wearing long sleeves. Had there been some terrible car accident or something where she'd lost her family, and maybe she had scars on her arms from the accident that reminded her of what she'd lost? He hadn't seen any scars today, but then again the cuffs that went with her dress were quite deep.

But she'd asked him specifically to steer clear of the subject. He couldn't push her any further. Not just now.

The pizza arrived; he cut it into slices while she got the salad out of the fridge. Funny how easy it was to be with her, he thought.

'Have you put that proposal together yet?' he asked when they were both sitting at her tiny kitchen table.

'Nearly. Have you heard anything from any producers?'

'I'm waiting for a few call backs.' He stopped abruptly.

She seemed to guess why, immediately. 'I'm not

going to leak anything, Liam. I wouldn't want to ruin any potential deals for you.'

'No, of course not. Sorry. I guess I'm a bit touchy about it.'

'Building your career up again from nothing, when you're used to being at the top—that's not easy. Especially when you know the whole world's watching you.'

He wasn't sure whether she was talking about him or her. Both, maybe. And that knowledge made him admit, 'I'm not dealing too well with that. I know I should be grateful for having a second chance, but at the same time I really resent having to start all over again, as if everything I achieved before just doesn't count.'

'People are rooting for you, Liam. They want you back on top again.'

'Maybe. But the media's fickle. One day you're a darling, the next you're a scapegoat.' He shrugged. 'There are a few people out there who'd like to see me fail.'

'You won't fail.'

The sincerity on her face touched him. She really did believe in him. Probably more than he believed in himself.

'It's just a shame you've been paired with the contestant who can't dance.'

He shook his head. 'You *can* dance, Polly.'

'Liam, don't flannel me. I know I'm hopeless. I

wanted ballet lessons when I was little, and my dad wouldn't let me. He said there was no point because I was too clumsy.'

He could see the hurt flicker in her eyes. She hid it quickly, but her smile went a touch brighter. 'I promise I'll try my hardest not to let you down, Liam.'

'Maybe the foxtrot didn't suit you. You're doing a lot better with the cha cha cha.'

She gave him a wry smile. 'I wasn't fishing for a compliment.'

'I know. You wouldn't have got one if you had been.' He raised an eyebrow. 'Nobody puts Polly in a corner.'

This time, she laughed. 'Yeah, yeah.'

It was easy to relax with Polly. Her warmth and sweetness made him feel different, tempting him to let his barriers down and let himself fall for her. Yet at the same time he knew she was vulnerable. She might be feeling the same way as he was right now, but she was the kind who wanted a settled forever, and he had no idea what his future held or whether, in a couple of months, he'd be living thousands of miles away. So he'd have to be careful not to step over the line. For both their sakes.

'It'd be pretty stupid to ask a cake fiend if he'd like some brownies,' Polly said, clearing their plates away. 'So I'll just say help yourself.' She put the plate on the table, and made coffee.

The brownies were surprisingly good. 'A hidden talent, Ms Adams?' he asked.

She shrugged. 'I like baking. I used to make these on Thursday nights for the team—Fridays were our day for shooting the pre-recorded stuff, so we always had Chocolate Fridays.' Her smile turned super-bright again, and he knew she was missing her old team. But then she gave him a wicked grin. 'That was your fourth. I thought dancers were leery of scoffing too many carbs?'

'You were counting? Right. I'll make you work hard for the rest of the week to burn them off.'

'Yeah, yeah.' She took another brownie.

So did he.

When Liam had finished his coffee, he kissed Polly on the cheek. 'Goodnight. Thanks for dinner.'

'Pleasure.'

He really wanted to linger. But it wouldn't be fair to either of them. 'See you in the morning for training.'

## CHAPTER SEVEN

On Thursday, they were halfway through training when the door opened.

'You have visitors,' Amanda announced.

Danny, Mike and Charlie rushed over to Polly and hugged her in turn.

'We've missed you, Pol,' Danny said, giving her another hug. He looked at Liam. 'Sorry for bursting in on your training session, but this woman's impossible to pin down.'

'We get all these lovely chirpy texts from her,' Charlie said, 'and we have no idea if she's faking it or not, because you can't really tell from a text, and she never answers her phone.'

'Because I've been busy,' Polly protested. 'And I'm fine.'

'We needed to see that for ourselves, Pol,' Mike said.

'I'm *fine*. Really. You all obviously know Liam.' She introduced the crew swiftly. 'Liam, this is Danny—now, if you were dancing with him, you'd win, because he's great—this is Mike, and this is Charlie.'

She was different with them, Liam thought. Relaxed. And she was clearly fond of all of them, because she seemed happy to be hugged and have her hair ruffled by them all. Hadn't she said that they were like the brothers she didn't have? Liam couldn't remember the last time he'd been that close to someone. Since the accident, he hadn't let anyone close— even family. And maybe that wasn't such a good idea, keeping himself separate and pushing people away. Being close to people made Polly sparkle.

'Sounds like a challenge,' Liam said. 'Show me what you've got, Danny?'

'Can I put some music on?' Danny asked.

Liam gestured to his stereo system. 'Help yourself.'

A few seconds later, a chart hit started pounding through the studio, and Danny gave them a demo of a street dance.

'Not bad,' Liam said when Danny had finished.

'A challenge, you said. Can you do that?' Danny put the track on again, and Liam mimicked what he'd seen.

'Not bad,' Danny said.

'I think we should record this for the *Step by Step* show,' Polly said. 'Are you up for it, Danny-boy?'

'It should be you doing the dancing, not me.'

'We can mix it up a bit,' she said with a smile.

She glanced at her watch. 'The cameras are going to be here in half an hour or so. If you don't have to be elsewhere, I could make us some coffee.'

'Polly, put the kettle on?' Charlie teased. 'Great. I'll give you a hand.'

Polly made coffee for all of them, including Amanda, who was thrilled to meet the rest of the *Monday Mash-up* crew. Especially when Danny promised signed photos for her children.

'We brought you this.' Danny handed her a bag of fan mail. 'I know we could've sent it to Shona, but we wanted an excuse to see you.' He looked at Liam. 'We weren't coming to check you out.'

'No?' Liam asked, knowing full well they were and raising an eyebrow.

Danny gave him a rueful smile. 'OK. A bit. Fliss—Polly's bestest friend—can't, because she's a teacher and she can't get the time off during the day.'

'Did she put you up to this?' Polly asked.

'Not answering that one, Pol.' Danny ruffled her hair and turned back to Liam. 'We saw the way you stuck up for her on the show, so we know you're good to her.'

Mike ruffled her hair. 'I like the hair, Shrimp. It suits you.'

'We really miss you on the set. It isn't the same without you,' Charlie added.

Polly grimaced. 'I couldn't stay, in the circumstances.'

'I know. We're all so angry with Harry. He's *such* an idiot,' Danny said.

'Don't give him a hard time. He couldn't help falling in love with her.' Polly couldn't quite bring herself to say Grace's name.

'I can't believe you're taking this so calmly,' Charlie said. 'Well, he's not putting her in your place.'

Polly flinched. 'Is that what he's suggesting?'

'We said we'd leave if he even thought about it,' Mike said. 'At the moment we have a series of guest presenters. People have auditioned for your job, but none of them's been like you.'

'Give them a chance,' Polly said. 'You need time to build the chemistry.'

*Chemistry*, Liam thought. He had a nasty feeling that was happening with him and Polly. And it rattled him. She was making him think differently. Making him feel again.

'We want *you* back, Pol,' Danny said, looking serious.

She shook her head. 'Not going to happen.'

'New job?' Charlie asked.

'Not even the sniff of an audition, right now,' she admitted. 'But I can't work on *Monday Mash-up* again.'

The boys stayed there for long enough to do some dancing for the cameras on *Step by Step*, and to tell all the viewers to vote for Polly.

'We'd better let you get on,' Danny said when the

camera crew had gone, and the three of them gave her a hug and kiss goodbye.

'They're nice lads. I can see why you miss them,' Liam said. 'But come on, you, back to work.'

She knew he'd seen the glimmer of tears in her eyes and guessed exactly why they were there. But there was also an additional guilty layer: the fact that she was missing the crew, but she wasn't missing Harry. And shouldn't she be missing the man she'd been going to marry?

On Friday, Polly was enjoying their last real practice of the routine. She loved the music. She'd always thought of herself as the girl-next-door type; but the way she was dancing with Liam made her feel sexy. More attractive than she'd felt in years. She lost herself in the dance, to the point where she ended up overbalancing on a spin. Liam caught her before she fell and pulled her against his body to steady her. 'OK?'

'OK,' she whispered.

Except she was aware of every drop of blood thudding through her veins, the way Liam was just that little bit too close, to the point where she could feel the rise and fall of his chest as he breathed. She could feel the moment that his breathing changed, became faster and shallower, and glanced up at him to see that he was staring at her mouth. A moment later, she was staring at his. Thinking. Wondering.

They were a whisper away from kissing. Just as they'd been at the club.

She felt hot all over. Maybe it was the music or the dancing, she tried to tell herself, but she knew that wasn't strictly true. It was Liam making her feel all hot and bothered. And she couldn't drag her gaze away.

But then Amanda opened the studio door. 'Sorry to interrupt. There's a phone call for you, Liam. It's Barney, that guy from the Broadway show.'

Liam set Polly on her feet. 'I'll be as quick as I can.'

'No worries. It sounds important.' Hadn't he said he wanted to work with a Broadway cast?

'It is, a bit. Thanks.'

Polly took advantage of the moment to splash her face with cold water. Yes, Liam Flynn was gorgeousness personified, and a really nice guy to boot, but she couldn't get involved with him. Even if it wasn't too soon after Harry, there were other things in the way. Liam wanted to work on Broadway when *Ballroom Glitz* had finished; this phone call sounded as if he was well on his way to making that happen.

She intended to stay in London. Long-distance relationships didn't work—she'd seen too many show-biz couples break up because of it. She wouldn't expect Liam to give up his dreams for her; but she wouldn't want to give up the security of her life in London for him, either.

So she just had to forget about that near-kiss. They couldn't get involved.

To her relief, Liam acted as if nothing had been about to happen when he came back into the studio, and they finished polishing the routine.

On Saturday, just before the dress rehearsal, Liam was waiting in the Green Room. He did a double take when Polly walked in. She looked stunning. OK, so he'd been there when she'd chosen the costume, but he hadn't actually seen her try it on. The tomboyish kids' TV presenter had morphed into a gorgeous, kittenish flirt. Especially when she practised one of the cha cha cha steps as she walked, making her hips sway. It was sultry and sexy as hell. The movement ruffled her swishy skirt, but it ruffled his composure even more.

'I had no idea you had such fantastic legs.' Annoyance with himself at the way he was letting her get to him made him snippy. 'Why do you always dress in awful clothes?'

'I don't dress in awful clothes,' Polly protested.

'Yes, you do. You have those shapeless long-sleeved T-shirts—and if you're not in baggy jeans, you're in shapeless black trousers.'

She lifted her chin. 'So you're saying I'm unfeminine?'

'No, I'm saying that you hide yourself and I don't understand why.' He lifted both his hands in a gesture of surrender. 'It's none of my business, I know, and if you're doing a kids' show I guess you need to dress the part.'

She sighed. 'Grace was feminine. That's what gave Harry the kaboom.'

If he didn't have such a tight rein on his emotions, he had a nasty feeling that she'd be giving *him* the kaboom. 'If Harry saw you wearing what you're wearing now, you'd give him the kaboom.'

'Three weeks ago, I would've wanted to hear that,' Polly said.

'And now?' Liam asked, his throat feeling scratchy.

'Now,' she said, 'it doesn't matter. I've had time to think. And you're right. I can't let my happiness rely on someone else. Only on me.'

This time, they were on third on the show. And Polly started smiling as soon as the music started. This time, the dance was over far too quickly.

The applause astounded her. As did the praise from the judges.

At the end of the show, they were in sixth place on the judges' leader board. Millie came over to her with a microphone. 'How do you feel, Polly?'

'Utterly thrilled that we're not bottom this week!' Polly said, beaming. 'I loved learning the cha cha cha.'

'And you hope that you'll be here next week?'

She nodded. 'I really want to stay in, because next

week is the waltz. I've always wanted to do that—whenever I've watched the show, the dancers looked so romantic in those floaty dresses.'

'If you want to see Polly Anna and Liam doing the waltz next week, phone up and vote for them!' Millie ordered the audience.

While they were waiting for the phone lines to close, the professional dancers did two numbers, and there was a chart act playing their last hit and the newest single.

Polly tried not to let her nerves get the better of her. This week was the first elimination. Even though they'd managed to stay out of the bottom two on the leader board, if the public hadn't responded to them and they ended up in the bottom two once the votes were taken into account they would be in the dance off.

'And now, the moment you've been waiting for—the results,' Millie intoned.

All the couples walked onto the stage and waited in their allotted spots, with a light fixed on each of them. Polly's heart was pounding so hard, she was sure the audience would be able to hear it.

Liam stood behind her with his arms wrapped round her. He dipped his head so he could whisper into her ear, 'Stop worrying. It doesn't matter if we end up in the dance off. You've done really well tonight and you *know* you can do it.'

'And the first couple who will be going to the

dance off tonight, in no particular order, are Jane and André.'

The next two names were a blur.

'Also going through next week—Polly Anna and Liam!'

For a second, Polly couldn't take it in.

They were through.

*They were through!* She whooped and mouthed 'Thank you' to the cameras, then spun round and kissed Liam as the spotlight above them switched off.

Liam's arms wrapped round her, holding her close.

And then his mouth moved against hers. Teasing her. Coaxing her. Tiny, nibbling kisses that made her press herself against him and tip her head back, changing the angle between them so he could part her lips and deepen the kiss.

*Kaboom.*

So this was what it felt like. As if her blood were fizzing through her veins. As if a thousand starbursts had lit up the sky. As if she were floating. And her senses were filled with Liam. The softness of his skin against hers, the citrusy scent of his shower gel, the warmth of his arms wrapped round her, the sweetness of his mouth.

She'd never, ever felt like this before, wanting the kiss to last until the end of time because it was so utterly, utterly perfect.

But then Liam stopped kissing her and Polly was horribly aware of a low catcall coming from Kyle, the footballer who was one place above them on the leader board.

'You two had better hope the cameras didn't catch that,' he said.

Oh, no. If *that* had been shown on national TV, the gossip rags would be going crazy. She and Liam had both had more than enough column inches about them for the wrong reasons.

She pulled back. 'Whoops. Guess I got a bit overexcited about getting through to next week,' she said lightly.

She couldn't meet Liam's eyes as the shame scalded through her. She'd just let him kiss her stupid onstage, in front of millions. Worse still, she'd incited it by kissing him in the first place.

How stupid was she?

'I—I'd better get changed. See you tomorrow,' she said, and raced off the stage, not wanting to face him again until she'd had time to cool down and get her common sense back.

# CHAPTER EIGHT

POLLY had a whole night to think about what an idiot she'd been. Not only had she let Liam kiss her stupid onstage, she'd fled afterwards, too flustered to face him. She hadn't answered her phone or a single text message. She'd just holed up in her flat, filled with panic about her recklessness.

OK, so this had been building up ever since they'd danced together at the club. Ever since he'd nearly kissed her in training. She'd known deep down that it would happen.

But she'd handled it really, really badly.

Would Liam have spent last night thinking about the way they'd kissed as the spotlight went off? Would he realise that she'd rushed off in panic? Or would he think she was capricious, treating him the way his ex had?

How would he react to her this morning?

She felt more nervous when she rang the bell to the studio than she'd felt at her first training session. Would he even answer the intercom?

'Come up,' he said, and pressed the buzzer to let her in.

She couldn't tell a thing from the tone of his voice; it was completely neutral. Her nerves increased as she walked up the two flights of stairs to the studio and opened the door.

When she entered the room, she couldn't tell a thing from his expression, but she knew she had to face up to this. Explain herself.

'About last night...' She stopped, not having a clue what to say. 'I'm sorry,' she mumbled.

'Uh-huh.'

Why did he have to be so inscrutable? Couldn't he help her out here, show some kind of reaction so she had some idea of how he felt—what *he* wanted?

'I guess I panicked.'

'I noticed.'

Was he angry? Hurt? Amused? She didn't have a clue. 'So what happens now?' she asked warily.

'It's like you said last night. You were overexcited about getting through. So was I.' He shrugged. 'These things happen. It doesn't mean anything.'

*It doesn't mean anything.*

She fought to keep her expression neutral. She'd felt the kaboom—but Liam obviously hadn't.

And that *hurt*.

No way was she going to let him know that. But she'd make very sure that from now on she regarded the dancing as strictly work and nothing more. She wasn't going to make the same mistake she'd made with Harry and fall for someone whose feelings weren't the same as hers. Even if right now she was too confused to know exactly what those feelings were.

But she could definitely smile her way through this one. 'I'm glad that's sorted,' she said, in superbright Polly Anna mode. 'Well, no rest for the wicked. We're starting the waltz today, aren't we?'

'Yes. Are there any songs I need to avoid, apart from the one I already know about?'

She shook her head. 'Just that one.'

'Good. Let's get started. The waltz is a little bit like the foxtrot, but there are three steps instead of four, and the rhythm's slightly different. Back, side, close—each for one beat.' He demonstrated the moves for her.

It looked easy enough. Then again, she'd had trouble with the foxtrot. She couldn't afford to get this wrong. Not if they were going to stay in the competition. Given that Liam might have a Broadway producer interested in his work, she owed it to him to get this right.

'I'm going to keep it uncomplicated this morning, until you're used to it. You'll be going backwards, and we'll dance anticlockwise round the room,' he told her. 'We'll bank round the corners for now, because I want you to get used to the rhythm of the dance before we add in the turns.'

He switched on the music; when the first notes of 'Moon River' floated into the air, her smile turned genuine. 'I know this one. *Breakfast at Tiffany's* is one of my favourite films.'

'You look like Audrey Hepburn, with your hair like that.'

No way was she as gorgeous and elegant as the actress, but the compliment warmed her—and flustered her at the same time.

Though that wasn't strictly true, she knew. The real reason she was flustered was Liam and her growing awareness of him. Did she feel this way just because they were spending so much time together? Or was it more than that? Guilt flooded through her. It was only a couple of weeks after she should've been getting married to Harry, and right now she couldn't really remember how Harry made her feel. But one thing she was absolutely sure about: he hadn't made her pulse skip the way Liam did. She'd never reacted this strongly to anyone before. Never felt the kaboom. She wanted to run away and pretend it wasn't happening; but at the same time she couldn't deny it. Part of her wanted to go for it; but part of her was too scared to risk it.

She could see that Liam was looking at her mouth, and suddenly she couldn't breathe. So much for what he'd said about it not meaning anything. She had the distinct feeling that he, too, was thinking about that kiss last night. That he, too, wanted to repeat it? That he, too, was feeling guilty and mixed-up as well as longing for a deeper intimacy?

Or was she just fooling herself?

He seemed to make an effort to pull himself together. 'I'll count you in for two bars. One, two, three; one, two three; now.'

And she stumbled.

It didn't help when he switched to saying, 'Left, right, together; right, left, together,' because all of a sudden she couldn't tell her left from her right again. And putting it all in time to the music was next to impossible.

'This is ridiculous—why can't I do it?' she asked when he went to change the music. 'Am I so stupid that I can't count to three?'

'No. With the foxtrot, you know you start with your right leg and it's always right, left, right, left. With the waltz, you have to concentrate a little bit more and remember which leg you moved back last time,' he said. 'But you managed to get the foxtrot and the cha cha cha, so have faith in yourself. You'll get this one, too.'

She tripped over him yet again. 'Sorry.'

'Don't apologise. And, no, before you ask, you haven't hurt my back. Let's keep going. You'll get there.'

At the end of the session, she was disappointed that he didn't suggest a late breakfast together; but it was probably best that they didn't spend time together outside the studio until she'd managed to squash these ridiculous feelings about Liam. He'd kept today strictly to teaching: which told her everything she needed to know. He didn't want to take things any further between them. And she wasn't giving him the chance to reject her. She still had her pride.

On Monday, Amanda came in to the studio, wagging a finger at them. 'Well, you two, you've certainly got everyone talking about you. All the boards are speculating about whether Pretty Polly and Luscious Liam are an item.' She paused, raising an eyebrow as she looked at them both. 'Are you?'

'No, we're not,' Liam said.

'You kissed each other,' Amanda pointed out. 'On national television.'

'I was thrilled to bits at getting through to the next round, that was all,' Polly protested. 'I kissed my driving examiner when I passed my test. And I kissed the guy who taught me to ride a unicycle. I kiss Mike, Danny and Charlie all the time.' If Polly was honest with herself though she knew that this kiss with Liam had been different.

'That's true. I saw you with them last week. Oh, and please tell them thank you for the photos. The kids were thrilled.' Amanda looked worried. 'Seriously, though, I've had a few calls from the press.

What do I say? Because I've tried "no comment" and they just keep asking.'

'Tell them I got overexcited and I kiss everyone,' Polly said. 'It didn't mean anything.'

Though she couldn't look Liam in the eye as she said it. She didn't want him to guess what she was starting to feel about him.

Polly really wasn't getting the hang of the waltz. By Wednesday morning, Liam was seriously worried. He'd tried doing a natural turn with her, and she'd stumbled over the steps. He knew that people often found one way easier than the other, so he'd tried the reverse turn with her instead—and that hadn't worked any better.

This was even worse than the foxtrot. If they didn't do the waltz the way the audience expected, all spins and twirls and glamour, the public wouldn't vote for Polly.

He switched off the music. 'We're struggling with this.'

'More than struggling. I really can't do this.' Polly lifted her chin. 'Look, I've been thinking about it. There's only one thing I can do now.'

'What's that?'

'I'm pulling out of the competition.'

'What?' Liam stared at her in disbelief. She couldn't be serious.

'I'm pulling out of the competition,' she repeated.

'You need to get the Broadway producers to notice you. If I mess things up for you on Saturday night and we're eliminated, they're going to blame you— it's because you're not good enough at teaching me and your choreography's too hard, so you'll make a mess of working with their cast.'

'I'm a perfectly adequate teach—' Liam began.

She held up a hand. 'Let me finish. In *their* eyes, we'll be eliminated because you're not good enough at teaching me or leading me, or you're trying to get me to do something too difficult. Whereas we know the truth—I'm just hopeless at this and I'm never, ever going to get it. We've been training for half a week now, and I can barely do the basic step, let alone the twirly bits. I hate coming here right now, because I feel so stupid and useless. I'm never going to be able to follow a routine. If I pull out of the competition, they'll know we didn't make the final because of *me*, not because of you.'

'That,' Liam said, 'is the most screwed-up logic I've ever heard. The reason you're not getting the waltz, Polly, is because you're panicking instead of concentrating on what you're doing.'

'I *am* concentrating. I just can't do it. Like my dad said, I'm a fairy elephant, not a fairy ballerina.'

Liam felt his temper bubble, and he wasn't sure what made him angriest. Polly's lack of self-belief— which he was beginning to understand, given what she'd just let slip; her ridiculous idea of pulling out of the competition; or the fact that he was calling her on her lack of concentration and knew he was being a total hypocrite because he was having problems concentrating, too. Every time she was in a ballroom hold with him, he thought back to Saturday night and that kiss. A kiss that had blown his mind because he'd never felt something so sharp and intense before, even with Bianca. A kiss that had made him put all his barriers back up because Polly was a real danger to his equilibrium.

'Your father was talking rubbish,' he said. 'And you are *not* pulling out of the competition. You're going to concentrate, Polly Anna Adams, harder than you've ever concentrated in your entire life, and you are going to learn the waltz. Properly.'

'Are you listening to a single word I'm saying?' Polly's face flushed with temper. 'I can't do this, Liam. I've tried and I've tried and I've tried, and I just *can't* do it. I'm never going to be able to do it. I hate this stupid dance. I don't want the judges to think it's your fault when it's all mine. So I'm pulling out of the competition.'

'Don't be so ridiculous,' Liam said.

She glared at him. 'Have you got a better idea?'

He glared back at her. 'Yes. We're getting out of here.'

She gave him a slow handclap. 'At last the man listens and realises I'm right.'

'You are *not* right. And we're staying in the competition. We're just getting out of the studio.'

'If you think taking me out to lunch is going to change my mind—' Polly began.

'I'm not taking you out to lunch. You're going back to your flat to pack an overnight bag and collect your passport,' Liam said.

She frowned. 'What? Why?'

'My better idea. We're going to dance somewhere else.'

She scowled. 'Don't tell me you're thinking tree-trunks. Though maybe that would work. I'll break my ankle so I can't dance on Saturday.'

'Don't be ridiculous. We're not dancing on a tree-trunk.' Though he did need to get a couple of things organised. Like now. 'You do have a passport?'

'Yes, but what's that got to do with dancing?'

'You'll see,' Liam said. 'And the waltz isn't a stupid dance. It's floaty and light and sparkly.' A lot like her. 'You're going to get this dance, Polly, whether you like it or not. I'll pick you up at your flat in an hour. Pack your dancing shoes. If there's any change to the schedule, I'll ring you.'

She stared at him, eyes narrowed. 'What exactly are you planning?'

'Changing your mindset,' Liam said. 'Don't argue. Just accept I'm right.'

'You are *so* not right.'

'I'm the teacher and you're the student. Which means you do what I say.'

She shook her head. 'You're full of it, Liam.'

He glanced at his watch. 'Get going, Pol. I have things to do.' When she remained stubbornly where she was, he added, 'If I'm wrong about this, then you can make me do any forfeit you like.'

'Any forfeit?'

He wasn't too sure he liked the sudden gleam in her eye; but if thinking about a forfeit stopped her thinking that she was useless and would never get the waltz, it would go a long way to sorting out their problems. She needed to start believing in herself. And he knew just the place to make it happen. 'Any forfeit. Now, *go*.' He shooed her out of the studio, then picked up the phone to make the arrangements.

Liam texted Polly to let her know he was on his way.

'So where are we going?' she asked when he arrived.

He refused to be drawn. 'It's a surprise.'

'Apart from the fact that I'm not wonderfully keen on surprises,' she said, 'I need to pay you for my plane ticket and my room.'

He shook his head. 'No, you don't—it's a teaching expense. And don't argue, Polly,' he said before she could cut in. 'I want you relaxed and calm.'

'How can I be, when I don't know what's going on?'

'I promise you'll like it.'

'I don't believe in promises,' she said. 'They're pie crust. Easily broken.' She'd learned that the hard way—firstly with her parents and then with Harry. People she'd trusted to keep her world safe, and they'd let her down.

'Mine aren't,' he said softly. 'Trust me.'

'Says the man who trusts nobody.' Which frustrated her no end.

'Wrong.'

'So who do you trust?' She damped down the flicker of hope that he'd say he trusted her.

'Myself.'

She rolled her eyes. 'You're impossible.'

'And your point is…?'

She gave up and stared out of the window for the rest of the journey.

At the airport, she realised where they were going as soon as their flight was called. 'Vienna?'

'Well, it's the waltz capital of the world,' he said. 'It's the best place to learn the dance.'

'Yeah, right.'

'Trust me. I have a friend there who runs waltzing weekends.'

'So you're getting someone else to teach me?'

'No. I'm calling in a favour and borrowing something from him.'

'What?'

'You ask too many questions, Pol.'

'I stand by what I said,' she grumbled. 'You're impossible.'

Though Polly enjoyed the flight, especially as Liam kept the conversation light and told her all about his favourite bits of Vienna. They caught a train from the airport into the centre of Vienna, then changed to the Tube; Polly noticed that Liam didn't even have to look anything up on a map, so clearly he'd done this plenty of times before.

Their hotel was a beautiful white building, half covered in ivy. Liam went to the reception desk, where he spoke rapid and fluent German; he returned with their room keys, and they went up in the lift to the top floor.

Their rooms were next to each other, and—despite the fact that the rooms were practically identical—Liam gave her the choice. The one she picked had a great view over the street, plus a wide, comfortable-looking bed.

She'd just about finished unpacking when there was a knock at her door.

'Ready?' Liam asked.

She nodded.

'Bring your dancing shoes.' He glanced at his watch. 'We're right on time.'

'For what?'

'To go to the ballroom.' He ushered her downstairs, handed in the key to the hotel reception desk and led her outside.

Waiting in front of the hotel was a *fiaker*, an old-fashioned open-topped carriage drawn by two white horses. The driver lifted his Derby hat at them. 'Herr Flynn?'

'*Ja,*' he confirmed, and turned to Polly. 'My lady, your carriage awaits.' He swept into a deep bow.

'Liam, I don't believe this!' She stared at him, stunned and delighted. 'When did you arrange this?'

'While you were packing. I told you I had things to do.'

'Wow. I feel like a princess.'

'That,' he said, 'is the whole idea.' He helped her into the carriage, then went round the other side of the *fiaker* to join her.

Inside the carriage, all Polly could really hear was the regular clop-clop of the horses' hooves on the cobbled streets. With the slight jolting of the carriage wheels on the cobbles, it felt as if they were in another time, not the twenty-first century.

She still couldn't quite believe that Liam had arranged a horse-drawn carriage to take them to the ballroom. Nobody had ever made her feel this special before, even Harry.

And then a really scary thought struck her. He'd said he meant her to feel like a princess. Was that the surprise? 'Are we going to a ballroom in a royal palace?'

'Not the Hofburg, if that's what you mean—but yes, the ballroom used to be part of a royal palace.

A royal summer residence.' He smiled. 'I guess it was kind of their garden shed. Albeit a posh one.'

Which told her nothing. Given the beautiful white stone buildings around them, she couldn't imagine a wooden shack stuck in the centre of the city. What would a 'posh garden shed' be like?

The carriage drew to a halt, and Liam helped her out.

They were in front of a stunning white stone building with three rows of tall windows, a green copper roof, and a circular room at each end topped with a green copper dome. Everything was lit up, and it looked stunning. Like a fairy tale.

'This is the palace?' she asked.

'It's a hotel, now. The ballroom's the, ahem, former garden shed. I would've booked us in here for tonight, but they didn't have any rooms available. I need to pick up the key from reception—Matt's left it for me—and get them to switch off the alarm.'

'Matt?' she asked.

'My friend who runs waltzing weekends.'

Liam had a conversation with the hotel receptionist in rapid German, then came back over to join her and led her through to the garden. At the bottom of the garden was a single-storey building, designed in the same style as the hotel.

'Quite some shed,' she said.

'It's even nicer inside.' He unlocked the door. From the hallway, she could see a large room with mirrors and gilding everywhere, and when he switched on the lights she was stunned by the huge crystal chandeliers.

'The room's not quite how I want it,' Liam said, 'but I'll sort that while you change.'

'Change?'

'Yup. Matt has lots of outfits for clients to use. I asked him to set out a couple of dresses in your size.'

'I can't believe you've arranged all this for me.' She really couldn't remember the last time anyone had done anything so nice for her. 'Thank you so much.' She wanted to hug him—but they weren't quite on hugging terms right now. 'Thank you,' she said again.

'My pleasure. This, Polly, is where you are going to get the waltz. Trust me. The ambience will make all the difference.' He led her to a side room where a suit was hanging up next to three dresses.

She looked at the dresses in dismay, realising that none of them had sleeves. How could she possibly wear one of them? Yet, at the same time, she knew that Liam had gone to a huge amount of effort for her. She couldn't be ungrateful and just throw it back in his face.

But he'd clearly seen the expression on her face and picked up immediately what the problem was. 'Sorry, I know you prefer long sleeves. I did ask for them. Or maybe there weren't any.' He looked stricken. 'This is all going horribly wrong.'

She swallowed hard. 'It's OK. I'll wear one of the dresses.' She knew she was going to have to be brave about this.

'No, it's fine. You can wear what you're wearing now to dance with me.'

'But you've gone to all this trouble.' And her casual clothes were going to ruin the ambience he'd carefully set up. 'I'll wear a dress.' There was a huge lump in her throat that made it hard to force the words out. 'I—I don't want to talk about it right now, but there's something I guess you need to know before I get changed.' She pushed up her sleeves, turned her hands palm-upwards and let him see the thin scars on her wrists.

He was the first person who'd seen them since Harry. She was aware that her hands were shaking slightly, and she couldn't look at him, dreading his reaction. Disgust? Pity? Neither option was one she wanted to face.

He said nothing, simply took her hands and raised her wrists to his mouth, then touched his lips very lightly to the scars.

She stared at him in shock. Now that she hadn't expected.

'Whatever made these happen,' he said softly, 'I'm not going to pry. If you want to talk later, I'll listen. If you don't want to talk, I'll respect that. And I'm not going to say a word to anyone. You don't need to worry about that.'

She noticed he hadn't used the word 'promise'—because what he'd just said went deeper than that. It was the truth. Honest and unvarnished. Something she could believe in.

'Thank you.' She could barely get the words out, she was shaking so hard.

'Wear the dress and don't worry,' he said. 'Because I don't see these.' He kissed the scars again. 'I see *you*, Polly Anna Adams. And you're beautiful.'

She felt tears pricking her eyelids. She wasn't going to let them leak out and disgrace her, so she gave him her widest smile instead. Best defence mode.

'Get changed, Pol,' he said softly. 'We're going to face the music. And dance.'

He took the suit and left her to change.

One dress in particular was irresistible; it had a navy blue chiffon skirt that finished just above the ankle, a lacy bodice and tiny spaghetti straps. Gorgeous and frothy—and the kind of dress she'd never dare to wear in a million years. She put it on, looked at herself in the mirror and, for the first time in half a lifetime, she didn't notice her wrists. The reminders of her shame and disgrace just vanished. All she saw was the dress.

She turned round, loving the way the skirt ballooned out round her. It reminded her a bit of the wedding dress she'd never got to wear, except she knew that Harry wouldn't have made her feel beautiful, the way Liam had. Harry never talked about her scars and had encouraged her to wear long sleeves all the time to hide them, clearly as ashamed of them as she was; Liam had made it clear he'd listen if she wanted to talk and wouldn't push her if she didn't.

Even so, she knew deep down that her scars would make a difference to the way he saw her. How could they not?

She fastened her shoes, then went back into the ballroom. And stopped dead. Liam had turned off the glitzy chandeliers and lit candles everywhere. Every single wall of the room was covered in mirrors; the light of the candles was reflected in them, and the reflections were reflected again, so the room felt as if it were full of stars.

Liam was wearing the suit and looked as gorgeous as he had at the dress rehearsal for their foxtrot. No, more than that, she thought, because the candlelight was much softer than the harsh studio lights.

This whole thing felt enchanted. If she was Cinderella, Liam was definitely Prince Charming. Except there was a lot more to him than just charm.

He smiled at her. And then the music started: a beautiful, simple tune in waltz time, played on a solo piano. Timeless. Perfect.

Liam held out his arms to her. There was no pity on his face, no censure; he was just asking her to dance with him.

She walked over to him and rested her left hand

on his arm, curling the fingers of her right hand over his—and then she was in hold and they were dancing to the music, in perfect time.

She didn't look at her feet or think about counting; she simply let him lead her round the dance floor, doing the basic step and banking round the corners to keep it simple. It was perfect.

And then somehow they were doing the turns—and this time it worked. This time, she could get the steps, and they were spiralling round with their legs sliding between each other's in perfect timing. Polly felt as if she were floating on air, but at the same time she was safe in his arms and she knew he wouldn't let her fall. It was the most amazing feeling she could ever remember, and she loved every second of it.

When Liam dipped his head to brush his mouth against hers, this time there were no cameras in the way, no catcalls to stop them. He caught her lower lip between his in tiny, nibbling kisses that made her mouth tingle. When she parted her lips, wanting more, he deepened the kiss; and she wasn't sure what made her feel more light-headed, the way he was kissing her or the way he was spinning her round and round on the dance floor.

Finally, the music stopped and Liam broke the kiss.

'We have to go,' he said softly. 'But do you get the waltz, now?'

She dragged in a breath. 'Just like you said. Sparkly and floaty.'

'Perfect.'

And she knew he wasn't talking just about the dance; his voice was husky and his eyes were dark and intense.

'Do you want to go out for dinner?'

He was giving her a choice. Go out to dinner and pretend this hadn't happened, or go back to the hotel with him.

She could put some much-needed distance between them.

Or she could give herself up to the magic of Vienna, the waltz and his kiss. Do what she really wanted to do. What she could see he wanted just as much as she did.

'I'm not hungry for food,' she said quietly.

Desire flared in his gaze. 'Me, neither.'

By the time they'd changed back into their normal clothes, Liam had locked up and they'd delivered the key back to the hotel reception, the *fiaker* was waiting for them outside. While they'd been dancing, it had started to rain and the driver had put the hood up on the carriage.

'Just you and me,' Liam said softly as the driver closed the door.

He kissed her all the way back to the hotel. When he'd picked up their keys, he kissed her in the lift. And in the corridor. By the time they reached her door, Polly was completely hot and bothered, wanting him more than she'd wanted anyone in her entire life. She needed to be skin to skin with him. Right now.

She could see in his face that it was the same for him.

'If you've changed your mind,' he said, his voice husky, 'tell me now.'

'I haven't,' she said.

He rubbed the pad of his thumb along her lower lip. 'Good.'

She unlocked her door.

And then he scooped her up in his arms and carried her over to the big, wide bed.

# CHAPTER NINE

POLLY woke the next morning, warm and comfortable. But her head wasn't on a pillow, it was on a male shoulder. And her arm was wrapped round a waist. A *bare* male waist.

For a moment, she was disoriented; but then she remembered where she was. In Vienna. With Liam. Who'd taught her exactly what the kaboom felt like, last night, and still had his arms wrapped round her.

She kept her breathing deep and even, hoping to buy herself some thinking time. Was he awake? His breathing was deep and even, too, but that didn't mean he was asleep. He, like her, could have just woken and realised the situation. He, like her, could be panicking and wondering what to do next. And he, like her, could be buying time by faking deep, even breaths.

So where, exactly, did they go from here?

Last night had been amazing. But it had been like something out of time. In their real lives, this couldn't possibly work. She knew Liam was going to be focused on his career, and she couldn't see quite how she'd fit into his life. How would he have time for her? If his dreams came true—and she knew he'd work hard enough to make sure they did—then he'd be in New York while she was in London. OK, so he might ask her to join him; but she'd know nobody in New York, and what was she going to do with herself while he worked crazy hours?

The sensible thing to do would be to call a halt to this. Now. Because otherwise she was just setting herself up for more heartbreak.

Liam couldn't remember the last time he'd woken with a woman's arms wrapped round him.

Well, he could. The night before the accident. And then he'd been in a hospital bed for weeks. When he finally came out of hospital, he and Bianca had slept in separate rooms because she'd claimed she was terrified of causing more damage to his back.

And then she'd walked out on him.

He'd had offers, since, but he'd turned them down gently. He wasn't interested in a meaningless fling, and he wasn't in the market for a relationship, so it had been easier to keep everything strictly platonic. Keep himself separate.

But Polly…Polly had really got under his skin. Even when she drove him crazy with that super-bright fake smile, her warmth and sweetness still drew him. And last night, she'd opened up to him. Shown him what she'd been hiding all along.

She was vulnerable. Fragile.

Yet, at the same time, she was strong. Liam knew she wouldn't have given up on him, the way Bianca had. She would've been there by his side all the way, cheering on his recovery.

And right now she was lying with her head on his shoulder and her arms wrapped round him. It would be oh, so easy to turn to face her. To kiss her awake, to watch her eyes open sleepily and then that warmth shine through at him. To tease her mouth with his until she responded, kissing him back the way she'd kissed him last night. Make love with her again until they were both sated.

Was she really asleep? Her breathing was deep and even, but he knew how often she faked her smile. Maybe she was faking sleep, too.

'Polly?' he whispered. 'Are you awake?'

There was a pause. Long enough to make him think that maybe he'd got it wrong. But then she whispered back, 'Yes.'

He shifted to face her. Still with his arms wrapped round her, and hers round him.

And he really couldn't help himself. He touched his mouth to hers. Gently. Lightly. His skin tingled at the contact, and every atom in his body was aware of her. How good she felt, close to him, soft and warm and sweet. 'Good morning,' he whispered.

'Good morning.' Colour bloomed in her face. She touched his cheek. 'You look like a pirate with all this stubble.'

'I feel like a highwayman,' he said. 'Ready to grab you from your carriage, lift you onto my horse, and ride off with you.' He kissed the corner of her mouth. 'And then I'd most definitely have my wicked way with you.'

'You'd look amazing in a highwayman outfit.'

So she had a highwayman fantasy, did she? Well, he could do something about that. Something that would be very, very satisfying for them both. 'I'm so talking to the wardrobe department.'

She shivered.

He could drown in those eyes. Especially when she was looking at him like that, her eyes wide and sultry. 'Polly,' he whispered. 'I want—'

She dragged in a breath. 'So do I. But we can't. We need to be sensible about this.'

'Sensible?' He went cold.

'Sensible,' she said again. 'We got carried away last night. And we shouldn't have done.'

He frowned. 'Polly, if it's about this…' He took her wrist and kissed the scar. 'It doesn't make any difference.'

'It's not about that.' But there was a catch in her voice and she pulled her wrist away. 'Liam, we're both picking up the pieces of our lives. We've both got a lot of baggage. If we let this go any further, it's going to get messy and complicated. Neither of us needs that right now. We need to concentrate on getting through the competition, so you can wow the Broadway producers and I can persuade a network to take a chance on me with another kids' show.'

She was right. Of course she was. But Liam had thought they'd shared something special last night. Clearly he'd been wrong. And it served him right for breaking his rule and not keeping himself separate.

'Yes,' he said, doing his best to sound cool and detached.

She blew out a breath. 'I'm sorry. I know I'm being a coward, but—'

'It's fine,' he cut in, not wanting to hear any more. 'We have a plane to catch, and I'd planned to take you for a proper Viennese breakfast, seeing as you worked hard enough to get the waltz right, yesterday.' He gave her a tight smile. 'I'll go back to my own room for a shower.'

'OK.' She sounded awkward.

Clearly she'd gone shy on him, even after what they'd shared last night. And when Liam dragged his clothes on, he noticed that she kept her back to him. Was she being courteous and giving him some privacy? Or was it because she couldn't face what they'd done? Or to stop herself being tempted? The way she'd kissed him this morning made him wonder.

A cold shower did a lot to restore his equilibrium and he managed to keep his face neutral when he knocked on her door. 'Ready for breakfast?' he asked when she opened the door.

She nodded. 'I've packed. Do we need to check out first?'

'No, we'll do that after breakfast.'

Liam took Polly to one of the oldest cafés in Vienna, where he knew the pastries were wonderful. Her smile was very bright, so he knew she was worrying that he'd push her to talk about those scars on her wrists. Well, he wasn't going to push her. He'd wait until she was ready to tell him.

'I'm having the Viennese specialty—Sachertorte and a *melange*.' At her questioning look, he said, 'Coffee. It's a cross between a latte and a cappuccino, without the cocoa on top.'

'Sounds good. And you're actually having chocolate cake for breakfast?'

'This is more than just chocolate cake.' He shrugged. 'This is Vienna. The cakes here are fantastic. There's a whole counter over there,' he said, indicating the glass-fronted display with all kinds of cakes and pastries. 'Go and find something you like the look of.'

She gave him a grateful look and escaped to choose some cake.

When the waitress brought their order over, he found that she'd opted for a rich strawberry torte, thin layers of soft sponge and strawberry mousse, topped with fresh strawberries and whipped cream.

'That looks lush.'

She tasted a forkful. 'It is. Want to try some?'

'Swap you for a taste of my Sachertorte?'

'Deal.'

Her smile was still a bit on the over-bright side, but Liam could tell she was starting to relax with him again. He enjoyed her feeding him a forkful of her torte, too; though he couldn't help thinking about last night and wishing things were different. He really was going to have to get a grip.

'A bit too rich for me,' was her verdict on the Sachertorte, 'but the coffee's fantastic.'

After breakfast, they headed back through the main streets.

'I can't believe how pretty it is here,' Polly said at the corner of Stefansplatz. She gestured to the gothic cathedral with its distinctive roof. 'Just look at that, the way the spire's so sharp against the sky.'

Liam had almost forgotten how much he loved Vienna, the wide streets and the incredible architecture and the art installations everywhere. Seeing it with Polly made him see it through fresh eyes.

'You're not the only one who likes it.' He pointed out the artists who were painting street scenes, with racks of pictures for sale set up by their easels.

A string quartet dressed in eighteenth-century costume was playing Mozart.

'Can we stop and listen for a while?' Polly asked.

'Sure.' And that was the other thing Liam loved about Vienna: the sound. The city of music. No out-of-tune buskers, here: whether they were string quartets or jazz trios or opera singers, they were all note-perfect.

They lingered until the piece ended, enjoying the music. And then the quartet started playing 'The Blue Danube'.

A waltz.

Liam glanced at Polly. Dancing in public would mean that she'd have to fake it. And that would make sure the physical awkwardness between them was gone before they went back to training. 'Recognise the tempo?'

Her eyes went wide as she guessed what he meant. 'We can't.'

'Sure we can. It's Vienna. People expect it.'

'But…'

He raised an eyebrow. 'Don't tell me you've forgotten the steps again?'

She lifted her chin. 'I have *not*.'

'Dare you.'

She held his gaze, and he knew she'd guessed he was calling her on something else. Then she nodded. 'You're on.'

Two seconds later, they were in hold and were waltzing along the wide street. Polly didn't miss a step, to his relief, doing the turns perfectly and keeping in time with the quartet. The tourists who'd stopped to listen to the music moved back slightly, giving them space to dance.

Everything faded for him except Polly and the music. Dancing to the slow, regular beat of the old tune. The rise and fall of their steps. Whirling her round, his leg sliding between hers and hers between his as they turned. Just like last night in the candlelit ballroom, when she'd looked up at him, those gorgeous brown eyes huge, and he'd dipped his head to kiss her.

It was too much for him to resist. He lowered his mouth to hers, his body on automatic pilot as he led her through the steps. His mouth was tingling where his lips touched hers—and then she kissed him back, her mouth sweet and responsive, making him feel as if they were dancing on air instead of in a wide, bustling boulevard.

It was a while before Liam realised that the music had stopped and people were clapping.

And he was still kissing Polly. Dancing to music that existed entirely in his head.

He slowed his steps to a halt and pulled back, noting the glitter in Polly's eyes and the hectic flush on her cheeks.

'Sorry,' he mouthed. Even though he wasn't.

'Bravo,' one of the onlookers called.

What else could he do but brazen it out? He bowed, and stood back as Polly dipped into a curtsey.

Dancing, he thought, could fix almost anything.

Except Polly's reservations. Because as soon as she stood straight again, all her barriers were back in place. Her eyes were filled with panic. And he didn't have a clue how to reassure her, because he was in exactly the same state.

They checked out of the hotel and took the train back to the airport to catch their flight. She was quiet all the way home, clearly brooding, and Liam had no idea how to reach her. All he could do, back in London, was to insist on seeing her home, right to her front door.

'Thank you. I didn't think I'd ever get the waltz. And what you did, setting up the ballroom like that...that was special.'

'Pleasure.'

She looked at him. 'I owe you an explanation. About...' She glanced down at her wrists.

Was that what she'd been worrying about, rather than the growing physical and emotional awareness between them? 'It's OK. You don't owe me anything.'

'Do you want to come in, um, for a glass of wine?'

He had a feeling that this was Polly's way of telling him she was ready to talk. And maybe what had happened with her wrists was the key to whatever was holding her back. Maybe if he understood that, he could make some sense of this whole thing between them. 'OK. That'd be good,' he said lightly.

She let them into her flat, dropped her bag in the hallway, ushered him into the kitchen and poured them both a glass of wine. Then she took a deep breath. 'Those scars are because I cut my wrists when I was fifteen.' She looked away. 'God, even saying it aloud makes me feel so ashamed.'

He'd already worked that out for himself, because she couldn't look him in the eye.

'I don't know how close you are to your family,' she said.

'On and off,' he admitted. 'They'd all rather I had what they call a sensible job, and they drove me crazy after the accident because they thought it was their chance to get me back on the straight and narrow. But they've come to accept that dancing's a big part of who I am—the better part. Although they're still not wonderfully happy about it, they're finally off my case about my job.'

That made her meet his eyes again. She looked shocked. 'But aren't they proud of you? Of all you've achieved, of the way you've made millions of people see beauty—the stuff you've choreographed for other people to dance, as well as the stuff you dance yourself?'

'In their own way, I suppose they are. And I guess it could've been worse. I don't think my dad could've handled it if I'd wanted to dance ballet. Billy Elliott, eat your heart out. Though I'm just as bad. I pushed everyone away after the accident.' He paused. 'So is this your way of saying you're not close to your family?'

'I'm an only child,' she said. 'Maybe it would've been easier if I'd had a brother or a sister. But I think I was probably a mistake. My parents…' She sighed. 'Let's just say they're not the greatest of role models. And I don't think they should ever have had children. When I was young, Mum was always leaving Dad because he was having an affair, and getting her own place for a while. She'd take me with her. I'd just get used to the new place, and then they'd make it up and she'd move back in with him.'

So Polly had never known any real stability, Liam thought. No wonder she was worried about getting involved with him. When his career took off again, he could end up taking a show round the world. Given what she'd said about her past, he knew she'd hate that kind of upheaval.

'It got worse when I was a teenager. Mum started having affairs to get back at Dad. The house was always full of fights and slamming doors. And they both yelled at me because I was so clumsy, always dropping things.'

And he'd just bet Polly grew clumsier every time she got stressed, making it a vicious circle. No wonder she'd said that she never screamed. She'd had more than enough of it when she was growing up. 'You were a kid. It wasn't fair to yell at you.'

'I guess it made a change from yelling at each

other.' She bit her lip. 'I hated living in chaos all the time. My teachers started asking me why my grades were dropping, and I was too ashamed to tell them it was because I couldn't concentrate. About how bad it was at home.' She swallowed. 'I asked Fliss's parents—my best friend's—if I could stay with them. Fliss had told them what was going on, and they said yes. I went home to pack. I was going to leave my parents a note to tell them where I was, but they found me packing. And they were so angry with me. They said I couldn't be friends with Fliss any more.' She dragged in a breath. 'I talked to Fliss at school, because they couldn't stop me, but I wasn't allowed to see her outside. And there was still all the shouting and the slamming doors and the leaving and the moving back in.'

Liam's heart ached for her. No wonder she'd done something so desperate. She must've been so unhappy. Sure, there had been rows at home—mostly over his choice of career—but he'd grown up knowing he was loved.

'In the end, I failed my mock exams. And I'd just had enough. I wanted out. I didn't know who to talk to, who could help me. So I…cut my wrists.' She swallowed hard. 'It was a cry for help. And I'm ashamed of it now.'

Even though part of him was yelling a reminder that he needed to keep himself separate, to keep his heart safe, right now Polly's need for comfort was greater. He couldn't stay away any more. 'Pol. I know we're not—well, together. But I can't just sit here and watch you rip your heart out like this. You need someone to hold you. And I'm here.' He stood up and went round to her side of the kitchen table, scooped her out of her chair, sat in her place and settled her on his lap, wrapping his arms round her.

'I don't know whether I want to weep for you most or bang your parents' heads together,' he said. 'And you're being way too hard on yourself.' He held her close. 'When you're fifteen, you have enough to deal with anyway, without having family troubles on top of that. Of course you'd have dealt with the situation differently at, say, eighteen, but you were only fifteen, Pol. You were still a kid. You couldn't be expected to cope with their mind games and self-ishness. And I'm sorry you had to go through that kind of unhappiness.' He paused. 'Obviously they found you in time after you did it.'

She nodded. 'They took me to hospital. The doctors patched me up and sent me for counselling. That's when I learned that smiling makes things better. Fake it until you make it.'

'You don't always have to put on a brave face. It's OK to be upset or angry.'

'No, it's not.'

He decided not to point out that she'd lost her temper with him and cried all over him. Right now she'd smile her way through anything he said. He'd thought he was stubborn, but she made him look like an amateur.

There was nothing he could say. He just held her. 'Did your parents finally wake up to what they were doing?'

She nodded. 'I think seeing all that blood shocked my parents into going for therapy, too, and the fighting and the leaving and the getting back together all stopped. But we don't really trust each other. They don't trust me not to go into meltdown every time something stressful happens, and I don't trust them to be there for me when life doesn't go the way I want it to.'

'You didn't go into meltdown over Harry. Well, except your haircut. Which I take was a statement that you were kind of reinventing yourself without him.'

'I did it myself with nail scissors. Just to get rid of the one thing Harry always said he loved about me, because—well, I was angry and hurt, and this was my way of lashing out.' She gave him a wry smile. 'Cutting off my hair to spite my face, you might say. Shona freaked out slightly because she knows about my past, but she dragged me off to get my hair fixed.'

'It suits you.'

'And it doesn't take two hours to dry any more. That's a bonus.'

Another of those wide Polly Anna smiles. He

stroked her face. 'I know Fliss and Shona have been careful with you. I take it your parents are treading on eggshells?'

Polly grimaced. 'Dad's first concern was the money. How much he'd paid out in deposits and would have to forfeit. And then Mum started shouting at him for being selfish.'

'Now I *really* want to bang their heads together. How can they put themselves first when your life's gone pear-shaped?'

'It's how they are.' She sighed. 'I guess I'm a coward, because I've been avoiding them ever since. But it's a lot easier dealing with them at a distance.'

'You're not a coward, Pol. You're sensible. I'd avoid them, too.'

She smiled wryly. 'I wish they were more like Fliss's parents. Fliss let me move in with her until I found a flat—and the second she told her parents what had happened, they came round to give me a hug and ask if I had a to-do list they could help with.'

Thank God she had someone in her life who cared enough for her. And he made a mental note to call his family later. He'd pushed them away too much; it was time he started appreciating them. They only interfered and nagged because they cared. He was lucky. 'Fliss's family sound lovely.'

'They are. Actually, Harry's parents are lovely, too. After he told them, they called me and told me he's an idiot, and just because I wasn't with him any more it didn't mean I couldn't still be part of their lives.'

Because to know Polly was to love her, Liam thought.

And he stuffed that thought right back in its box before it had a chance to grow. Love? He wasn't in love with her. Love wasn't something he did any more. Besides, Polly had made it clear she didn't want that from him. She didn't need that extra pressure right now. And he didn't need the complications.

He stroked her hair. 'I'm glad you've got good people in your life.'

'I have. I'm lucky. I have so much to be grateful for.'

'Or to make up for your parents,' he said.

She blew out a breath. 'I promised myself I'd never end up like them. That I wouldn't marry someone I'd fight with all the time and who'd cheat on me. That I'd only marry someone really stable. Someone I liked, someone who liked me back. Someone *safe*.'

'Harry?'

She sighed. 'And how wrong I was. He wasn't safe at all. He liked me, but he didn't *love* me. Not in the right way. I didn't realise he wanted the ka-boom. I thought liking him and feeling safe with him was enough—for him as well as for me. That it could be perfect.'

Fake it until—but they *hadn't* made it, had they? And no doubt that had shaken Polly's faith in herself even more. 'I take it you didn't feel the kaboom for him?' Liam asked gently.

She shook her head. 'So I guess he was right to call it off, because it wouldn't have worked. Not in the long term. What we had wasn't perfect. I was kidding myself, because I wanted it so badly. In the end he probably would've ended up cheating on me, because we loved each other as friends. He needed more than that. And he's obviously found it in…' Saying Harry's new love's name was clearly a struggle, but she didn't shirk it. 'In Grace.'

Liam kept his arms wrapped round her, and Polly rested her forehead against his chest. 'Thank you. For not judging me.'

'I think you've already judged yourself much more harshly than anyone else could or would,' he said softly. 'So, no, I wasn't going to judge you. There's that old saying about walking a mile in someone else's shoes before you judge them. That's pretty true.'

'Maybe.' She closed her eyes. 'About last night— I'm sorry. I wish it could be different. It's the wrong time. If we'd met maybe in six months' time…'

'I know. But we didn't. So we'll keep this strictly colleagues. Friends,' he said. 'Don't worry. And I'd better let you get some rest. See you tomorrow.' He kissed her cheek. 'Call me if you can't sleep, OK?'

'Thanks.' She dragged in a breath. 'That's more than I deserve.'

'No, it isn't.' And how he wanted to kiss her properly. To kiss away all the pain and the heartache, let her lose herself in him. Take her to the edge of paradise, where nothing else mattered but each other.

But that wouldn't be fair to either of them. 'I'll see you tomorrow.'

And, although his heart was screaming at him to stay right where he was, his head was in control. He did what he knew was the right thing. And left.

# CHAPTER TEN

'WE'RE adding a small intro to the routine,' Liam said on the Friday morning. 'Because dance isn't just random movement—it should also tell a story.'

'And the story here is what?' Polly asked.

'I'm a guy from the wrong side of the tracks. I can't resist you, and you're—well.' He shrugged. 'Listen to the lyrics and you'll get it.'

She didn't. They were dancing to a romantic song, but that was it, as far as she was concerned. 'Colour me stupid and explain,' she said. 'Otherwise the audience is only going to get half the story, because I don't have a clue what I'm doing.'

'That, Pol, is the point. Just be yourself and dance with me. Now let's go through it again. You stand in the middle of the room and wait for me, and when the music begins I'll dance over to you and we'll move into ballroom hold.'

'The vee and the butterfly, right?'

'Right.'

When they stopped for a break, Amanda came in

with two mugs of coffee and a magazine. 'I've had more calls from the press this morning. And there's a story about you in *Celebrity Life*.' She opened the magazine and showed it to them.

The headline ran, 'Is Luscious Liam the one to make Pretty Polly smile again?', and there was a picture of them together in the café, seemingly gazing into each other's eyes.

'For pity's sake. I'm not going to make the poor girl dance for hours without a break. And don't they realise that you need regular refuelling if you're burning up calories in training?' Liam said, rolling his eyes. 'I hate that magazine.'

Especially because he knew he wasn't going to be the one to make her smile again. This felt like rubbing it in.

'They'll find someone else to talk about soon enough,' Polly said, flapping a dismissive hand.

'Um, the boards are all lively again this morning, asking the same thing,' Amanda pointed out.

'The answer's the same. We're just colleagues. Friends,' Polly said.

'Absolutely,' Liam agreed.

At the end of the training session, Polly was scheduled to sort out her dress in the wardrobe department.

'Do you want me to come with you?'

'No, I'm fine.' Though she knew why he was

being so protective. 'I've managed OK so far with the wardrobe department,' she reminded him gently.

'Does Rhoda know why you want long sleeves?'

She shook her head. 'I just told her I'm superstitious.'

He smiled. 'Which you're not, but the wardrobe department is used to prima donnas making ridiculous demands. Though you're nice, rather than demanding, so I think they'll indulge you. OK. Go and find something you love.'

'I take it you're in traditional ballroom dress?'

'Whatever you pick, it won't clash with what I'm wearing,' he reassured her.

In the wardrobe department, there was a dress that reminded Polly of the one she'd worn in Vienna, except it was white. And it came with long white fingerless gloves. Perfect.

'Liam rang when you were on the way,' Rhoda told her as she pinned up the hem of the gown. 'He asked if you could wear a tiara.'

'A tiara?' Polly blinked in surprise.

'He's right. It'll look gorgeous with that dress. And I'm pretty sure I have a fake diamond collar that'll go with it, too,' Rhoda said through a mouthful of pins. 'Hang on a sec.' She finished pinning up the dress, then went to look for the tiara and collar.

Polly waited while Rhoda made a few adjustments, then looked at herself in the mirror. 'Wow. This doesn't look like me.' Could she really be that elegant? The nude-coloured dancing shoes made her look as if she were dancing in bare feet. She looked like some kind of princess. The fairy ballerina she'd wanted to be, as a child—and Liam was the one who'd taught her how to dance lightly instead of clumsily.

'Perfect for the waltz,' was Rhoda's assessment.

Polly hugged her. 'Thank you so much. I wouldn't have had a clue where to start. You've been brilliant.'

'It's my job,' Rhoda said, but the sparkle in her eyes told Polly that she was pleased to be appreciated. 'Now you go out there tomorrow night and knock their socks off.' She patted Polly's shoulder.

'I'll do my best,' Polly promised.

At the dress rehearsal, Liam just stared at her. 'Wow. You look amazing.'

Polly smiled. 'Thank you. Let's just hope my dancing will be up to it.'

'It will be.'

He believed in her. Really believed in her.

If only she'd had the courage not to back away from him again that morning. But she hadn't. Still didn't.

When the show was underway, Liam disappeared briefly from the Green Room; Polly assumed it was for a comfort break, but then he reappeared just before Millie announced them. And her chin almost hit the floor.

He wasn't wearing the tailcoat, white shirt and white tie any more. He was dressed like a highwayman in breeches, a domino and a cloak.

Her mouth went dry as she remembered Vienna and her fantasy of him as a highwayman. His fantasy of scooping her from her carriage, riding off into the sunset with her, and having his wicked way with her. Oh, help. He flustered her so much that she could barely move, let alone dance.

'Liam?' Her voice was croaky.

'Trust me.' He winked at her. 'There's just a tiny extra bit just before the intro that we haven't practised.'

'Not practised?' Panic flooded through her. She was going to mess this up. Clumsy, geeky Polly was going to make a fool of herself, yet again.

'Just me,' he said softly. 'You're not dancing that bit. Trust me. Just react…well, naturally.'

'What are you up to?'

'Adding a little extra to the story.' He grinned. 'Being a bad boy.'

And how. That costume made her knees weak and her heart feel as if it had just done a somersault.

'Dancing the waltz to "Need Your Love So Bad", it's Polly Anna Adams and Liam Flynn!' Millie called.

Liam kissed her on the cheek just before they reached the stage. 'Just enjoy this and remember how it felt in Vienna.'

Polly went hot all over. Did he mean dancing in that amazing candlelit ballroom, or did he mean when they'd made love? When she'd woken in his arms?

Right at that moment, she wanted to throw caution to the wind and forget about having the perfect life. Liam wasn't perfect. But he made her feel special. And when he'd waltzed with her in the candlelit ballroom in Vienna, she'd lost a bit of her heart to him. Enough to let him close. And right now she wanted Liam. Wanted him kissing her. Wanted him making love with her. Wanted him making her forget everything except him.

She went to the starting position in the middle of the floor, waiting for him, as they'd practised. But then Liam came in on a whirl of dry ice. He fired a gun into the air, and there was a burst of fireworks.

The audience jumped and gasped—and so did Polly, putting her hands to her face in shock. This wasn't part of the routine. He'd said something about adding a little tiny bit to the intro…but he hadn't mentioned anything about dry ice and fireworks and gunshots. At all.

Then the music began. Liam pulled off his cloak, got rid of that and the replica gun, and promenaded towards her. Polly's heartbeat slowed fractionally as she recognised the beginning of their routine; she knew what she was doing now.

He took her hand, then spun her into his arms and the dance they'd actually practised began.

And now she got what he meant about the lyrics. He was the bad boy highwayman falling for the society princess, telling her how much he needed her love and why.

The highwayman she'd compared him to when she'd woken in his arms. The one who was so going to have his wicked way with her. The one who'd made her feel amazing. The one who was stealing her defences away a little bit more with every dance step he taught her. The one who was making her fall in love with him.

At the end, Liam bowed deeply and kissed her hand. The audience went wild, cheering madly. And Millie was fanning herself, teasing them both, as they went over to the judges' table.

Tiki, as usual, criticised them.

Scott rolled his eyes at her. 'I think it was incredibly romantic. Well done.'

'I loved it, too,' Robbie said. 'What a story. I love the idea of the highwayman falling in love with the society lady—and what a fabulous costume. Liam, you've got every woman in the place swooning. Where did you get the idea?'

Liam just gave an enigmatic smile and Polly really hoped her face was nowhere near as red as it felt. The last thing either of them needed was for people to know what had happened in Vienna. That was *private*, and she didn't want the gossip rags pulling it apart and making it sound tacky when it had been so very, very special.

When the scores came in, there were good marks from Scott and Robbie, and a rather more grudging one from Tiki. But they'd moved up another position on the leader board, and to Polly's relief the audience kept them out of the dance off again.

'How's your juggling?' Liam asked on Sunday morning.

'A bit rusty, but retrievable. Why?'

'Because I was thinking of a circus theme for the routine—we can start with you juggling, then go into the jive. And we could wear ringmaster-type costumes.'

She smiled. 'That sounds fun.'

'Which is what the jive is all about. OK. The timing's not what you're used to—it's one, two, three-and-four, five-and-six. But you've done one or two of the steps before, so it won't be a total nightmare.'

Knowing that he was going to talk her through the moves as he demonstrated, she sat down, making herself comfortable.

'Rock, rock, chassé left, chassé right,' he said, walking it through as he talked.

How did he do that? He made the steps look fluid and effortless. Beautiful. And his voice…he could've been reading the telephone directory, and she would still have been enchanted.

She pushed the thought away. They'd agreed to keep it strictly friends.

'It's a little bit like the cha cha cha,' she said.

'A little bit. And you're good at the cha cha cha,' he reminded her.

Then it was her turn to practise it. Liam stood behind her, guiding her movements with his hands, and it made her feel hot all over, remembering what his hands had felt like against her bare skin. To her surprise, she picked it up more easily than she'd picked up the waltz. And when he got her to do an underarm turn, she laughed. 'This is definitely like the cha cha cha.'

Polly spent the mornings practising dancing and the afternoons practising juggling.

On Tuesday, halfway through their training session, Amanda interrupted them.

'Call for you, Liam.'

He frowned. 'I'm working. Can I call back when Polly and I are done?'

'No. It's important—it's Barney. The guy you've been waiting to call you back.'

'The producer guy?' Polly asked. 'Go and take the call, Liam. I can amuse myself for a bit. I could even teach Mand how to do some juggling.'

'Thanks.' Liam gave her a grateful look.

When he returned, he switched the music back on. 'OK. Let's practise the changes again.'

'Not so fast. Does that call mean you're going to New York?'

He shook his head. 'Barney happens to be in London this week. He wants to meet me for a discussion—an audition, I suppose. He's going to call back later today with a time.'

'Move my training if you need to,' Polly said immediately. 'You have to talk to him and let him see how good you are, and that you can talk a dance as well as dance it.'

Liam was warmed by her faith in him. 'Thanks.'

'But you also have to meet me for lunch or dinner afterwards,' she said, 'and tell me all about it.'

'It's a deal.' And Liam had to remind himself that they'd agreed to be just friends. Being with Polly felt like more than that. Right woman, right place…

…and wrong time.

For both of them.

On Wednesday, Liam had an audition booked in the late afternoon. He'd already given Barney an idea of the costumes and the intent of his choreography; he'd also prepared a minute each from three different routines, which he'd dance himself.

All he could do was hope that the producer liked his work.

About an hour after Amanda had left, the buzzer went.

Was this Barney, arriving early to see how he coped with pressure? His heart was in his mouth as he answered the intercom. But it turned out to be a delivery boy.

He opened the parcel to discover a box of chocolates. Super-posh ones.

There was a note with it. *Sugar rush in case you need one. Better than cake. Good luck! Just be yourself and he'll realise how good you are. And you are SO getting that job. Polly x*

Liam couldn't remember Bianca ever having faith in him like that, and it really touched him. He grabbed his mobile phone, about to call Polly and thank her, when his intercom went again. This time it really was the Broadway producer.

There was no time for anything else. He'd call Polly later. He took a deep breath, and headed downstairs to meet the producer at the door.

After Barney had left, the first thing Liam did was call Polly.

'Thanks for the chocolates. They were lovely.'

'My pleasure. How did you get on with Barney?'

Liam blew out a breath. 'He has other people to

see this week, so I just have to wait and see.' Which wasn't high on his list of favourite occupations.

'Want to have dinner and tell me all about it? I mean, I know I'm not going to understand what you're talking about in the same way that a fellow choreographer would, but I'd still like to hear.'

He loved the fact that she was actually interested in his work. And so enthusiastic. 'That'd be good.'

He arranged to meet her at a pizza place just round the corner from hers. True to form, she was dead on time. They ordered their meal and a bottle of white wine, and he told her all about the audition.

'So this is the job you really, really want?' she asked when he'd finished.

'It's the job of my dreams, yes,' he admitted.

'I'll keep all my fingers crossed for you—but your passion for dance shows through when you talk, and the producer must've seen that. I'd pick you if I wanted something choreographed. I love the routines you do for the professional dancers on *Ballroom Glitz*.'

'Thank you.'

They didn't stop talking for the rest of the evening, and Liam was surprised by how late it was when he saw her home.

'Do you want to come in for coffee?' she asked.

Yes, but what he really wanted wasn't on offer and he wasn't going to push her. 'It's a bit late,' he prevaricated. 'You need to get some rest because I'm going to make you work incredibly hard tomorrow.'

He kissed her goodnight on the cheek, and just stopped himself pulling her into his arms and kissing her properly. But all the way home, he couldn't help wishing that he had. That he'd kissed her until those gorgeous brown eyes grew drowsy with pleasure. And then done it some more.

Thursday was another day of training, but Polly and Liam didn't get away with just sending a training video to *Step by Step* that week; they were called in for a live interview.

'So I really have to ask you the question that's all over the show's message boards and all over the celebrity news pages,' Jessica, the interviewer, said. 'Are you a couple?'

'No. We're friends,' Polly said. 'Good friends.'

'But I hear that Liam whisked you off to Vienna last week.'

'Because it's the waltz capital of the world. The best place to learn how to dance the waltz.'

But then she made the mistake of thinking about how he'd kissed her in the ballroom and carried her to his bed, and she went hot all over.

Jessica smiled. 'Polly Anna, my love, take my advice—*never* play poker. Your face is a dead giveaway.'

'We really are just good friends,' Polly protested.

'Absolutely,' Liam agreed.

'And we all know what "just good friends" means,' Jessica said.

'It means Liam's a great teacher and I have a lot of respect for him. He knew I just wasn't getting the waltz, so we just went to practise somewhere different, and it worked,' Polly said.

'But there's all that chemistry between you. He kissed your hand at the end of the routine.' Jessica sighed. 'It was the most romantic thing I've ever seen on the show.'

'That was all part of the dance story,' Liam said.

'Let's have a closer look,' Jessica said, and played a clip from their waltz the previous week. 'It's the way you look at each other,' she said. 'What do we think, audience? Are they a couple?'

'Yeah!' the audience chorused.

'Honestly, we're just friends,' Polly said.

If only she had the courage to change that.

But she'd turned Liam down. He was about to be busy with a new career that would mean he had practically no time for anything else, and she was scared of making another really bad decision that would turn her life into chaos again. It was better to be safe than miserable—wasn't it?

The dress rehearsal went well on Saturday. Polly absolutely loved their costumes. She was hot and sweaty by the end of the dance and almost breathing too hard to talk, but she was really happy.

They'd drawn the first slot that evening.

Millie announced them: 'Dancing the jive to "Johnny B. Goode", it's Polly Anna and Liam!'

Wearing ringmaster-style dress, she and Liam marched onto the stage to the tune of 'March of the Gladiators'. They started off with a couple of seconds of Polly juggling; everyone clapped. Then she threw each ball to Liam; he removed his top hat and caught the balls in the hat, pulled out a bunch of flowers from his hat and threw them to her. Polly caught them and bowed to him.

Then Liam pulled the Velcro tabs of her trousers to reveal a pair of sparkly shorts. The hats, trousers and props went; the music segued into the intro to 'Johnny B. Goode', and they started the jive.

Polly was enjoying every second of it—OK, so it was a fast dance and it was really hard work, but it was great fun and she loved being able to use her juggling skills again. Breathless, she glanced at Liam and he winked at her. Clearly he was enjoying this as much as she was, with all the high kicks and leg flicks. She smiled back at him.

But then she made the mistake of glancing into the audience.

In the second row, she saw Harry. With his arm round Grace's shoulders and his hand very firmly in hers.

*Harry and Grace.*

It was the first time Polly had seen them together as a couple—the first time she'd seen Grace publicly replacing her—and it threw her. She slipped, the routine completely gone from her head.

Liam picked her up and twirled her round, but Polly had lost where she was in the routine. She stumbled again when he put her down, and missed the next step.

Why was Harry here? And why had he brought Grace with him? Surely he'd know that she'd see them and it would put her off?

Maybe it had been Grace's idea, because she knew Harry wouldn't be that thoughtless. Polly was pretty sure that this was Grace's way of showing her that she and Harry were a couple now, and that if Polly had any mad ideas about showing off on the dance floor to get Harry back then she'd better forget about it. And Grace, being Grace, would've couched it another way, saying that it was showing support for Polly; Harry, no doubt still feeling guilty about the way he'd broken off their wedding, would've agreed to that.

Polly felt too sick to listen to the judges' comments. And she had no idea how she managed to walk off the stage to the Green Room.

But she wasn't surprised by how low the judges marked them. Or that as each couple went onstage for their slot their marks were higher than hers and Liam's.

Tonight could well be the last time she ever danced with Liam. She'd ruined everything—for him as well as for herself. And it was all her own stupid fault for not ignoring Harry and Grace.

'I need some air,' she muttered, and headed out to the corridor.

Liam followed her. 'So what happened out there?'

'I slipped.'

His eyes narrowed. 'You went white first. And it wasn't just a slip. You missed a few steps.'

'I—' She grimaced. 'I got distracted.'

'By?'

She knew she owed it to Liam to be honest, because she'd messed it up. Big time. 'Harry was there.' She bit her lip. 'With Grace.'

Harry.

She'd been distracted because she'd seen the man who'd let her down. The man who'd dumped her publicly for another woman only days before their wedding. The man who'd left her to pick up the pieces... And she was clearly still in love with him, whatever she said, or she wouldn't have let him distract her so she messed up the dance.

All that hard work, for nothing.

Though Liam knew that his anger wasn't only fuelled by the waste of their time and effort. He was searingly jealous, because Harry the Deserter could still affect Polly more than Liam ever could. And that made him angry with himself for being jealous in the first place. What kind of fool was he, wanting a woman who didn't want him? Hadn't he learned from his mistakes with Bianca?

'You're supposed to be working and not letting things distract you,' he said tightly.

'I just wasn't expecting to see them.'

'They could've been wearing clown suits and juggling firebrands while riding on a unicycle on top of a tightrope, and you still should've ignored them and concentrated on what you were doing.' He shook his head in disbelief. 'We've spent hours training for tonight, we had a great routine going, and you lost it all in a couple of seconds because you let your concentration go.' Because she was still in love with a man who didn't deserve her.

'I'm sorry.'

'Sorry isn't good enough, Polly. We're bottom of the leader board. And, no matter how much the public loves you, we're in the fourth week of the show. Halfway through. They're not going to let you go any further if you can't deliver. I'm pretty sure we're going to be in the dance off tonight.' He folded his arms. 'So what are you going to do, let Harry and Grace put you off again?'

She looked hurt, and then angry; colour flared in her cheeks. 'No.'

'How do I know that? How do I know you're not going to let this whole thing go because of your precious Harry? How long are you going to wallow in it, Polly?'

'I'm not wallowing.' She glared at him. 'And you've hardly got room to talk. You haven't dated since Bianca left you. And that's, what, a year?'

No, he hadn't dated anyone. But he'd slept with Polly. He'd let her way, way too close. He'd let her get under his skin in a way he'd never expected, and it threw him again now. He snapped back at her, 'Bianca's got nothing to do with this.'

'Neither has Harry.'

He glared back at her. 'No? So which of us messed up the routine after seeing the ex? I'm pretty sure it wasn't me.'

She lifted her chin. 'Wouldn't it throw you if you saw Bianca with—with—whatever his name was?'

'Tomàs. No. Because when I'm out on the dance floor, I'm focused on what I'm supposed to be doing. Entertaining the audience. Getting through the routine—and doing it well.'

She lifted her chin. 'Well, aren't you the smug one?'

No. He wasn't smug at all. He was furious. With himself, for starting to fall for a woman who was still in love with her ex. And with her, for still loving a man who'd treated her that badly. And the look in her eyes ripped the guard off his tongue. 'Bet-

ter smug than a wimp,' he rapped back. 'And now
they're both going to feel sorry for you. Poor Polly,
who's still so in love with Harry that she can't concentrate when he's in the room, even though he's
only got eyes for somebody else.'

'Go to hell,' she said.

'Because you know it's true.'

'No, it's not. I can concentrate.'

'Then prove it,' he said. 'When we get called out
there for the dance off, you damn well *prove* it,
Polly Anna.'

'Fine,' she said, glaring back at him. 'I will.'

'Good.'

Polly was still fired up and angry with Liam when
they were standing under the spotlights, waiting
to hear their fate. It barely registered when Millie
called their names as the first couple in the dance
off.

So Liam thought she couldn't do it? That she
couldn't put Harry out of her mind?

Well, she'd show him.

And how.

# CHAPTER ELEVEN

POLLY had her brightest, most dazzling smile in place as they were called out to the dance off. She completely ignored Harry and Grace. And this time the dance was perfect. Absolutely perfect.

At least, technically. It had lost all the fun and enjoyment of rehearsals and the first half of their dance, the first time round that evening. The bit before she'd let Harry and Grace wreck her concentration.

Scott praised her for getting it right, Robbie was his usual enthusiastic self, and even Tiki grudgingly said it was an improvement.

And then it was time for the judges to choose who they'd save. Who was going through to the next week of the competition.

Was this it? Would things end with Liam on such a sour note?

Everything seemed to be happening as if she were swimming through treacle. Impossibly slowly and long drawn-out, to the point where it was almost unbearable and she wanted to march over to the judges, shake them, and tell them to put her out of her misery *now*.

Tiki chose to save Imogen, the model; no surprises there, Polly thought.

Robbie was next to choose. 'I'm saving Polly Anna.'

So it all hinged on Scott.

He seemed to take for ever. But finally, he said, 'I'm saving Polly Anna.'

*She and Liam were through.*

Polly closed her eyes, then mouthed 'Thank you' to the judges. Somehow she kept her knees from sagging in relief, and walked off the dance floor with a smile she really didn't feel. Hopefully nobody would notice that she was faking it.

Afterwards, in the corridor, Liam caught her hand. 'Pol. We need to talk.'

Right now, she didn't want to talk to him. She was still angry with him, especially for what he'd said to her about wallowing. And she didn't want to stick around here, just in case Harry decided to seek her out and say something; the last thing she wanted was for Harry to realise that he'd put her off. She wanted to be out of the studio as soon as possible. 'I think we've already said it all, don't you?'

'No.' Liam's mouth thinned. 'We can't talk here; there are too many people to overhear us. Your place or mine?'

'Neither.'

'That's not an option.'

She knew he was right. If she walked away or caused a scene here, the gossip rags would find out and they'd be sure to speculate. 'Mine, then,' she said grudgingly.

'Right. Meet you out here when you're changed.'

She changed swiftly, returned her costume to Rhoda in the wardrobe department, and met him in the corridor.

'I've got us a taxi,' he said. 'It's waiting outside.'

They remained in awkward silence all the way to her flat until she closed her front door behind them.

'I'm sorry for what I said,' Liam told her.

Over the journey, she'd had time to think a bit more and her anger had simmered down. 'You had a valid point. I should've ignored them.'

'I stand by that bit. But not all that stuff about you wallowing in it and being a wimp.' He sighed. 'I guess I was angry that you're still so in love with Harry that you let it put you off. You're worth more than him, Polly.'

'I don't want to discuss Harry with you.'

'I guess not.' He paused. 'We have three weeks left of the show.'

'*If* we get through.'

'If.' His face was unreadable. 'Do you want to call it a day?'

'I don't know,' Polly admitted. 'I'm still angry

with you. But we've got this far. I want to prove to myself that I can do it.'

'I could say I've injured my back and let one of the others take my place. André, maybe.'

'He'd be even worse than you. Anyway, if Barney thinks you've injured your back, it'll lose you that job.' She sighed. 'I guess we have to pretend this didn't happen.'

'Fake it until you make it?'

'Don't knock it. It works.'

He raised an eyebrow. 'You're faking it now. Was it the first time you'd seen them together?'

'Since it happened? Yes.'

'Then it's understandable that it'd upset you. And I was unfair to you. I'm sorry.'

He meant it, she could tell. 'Apology accepted.'

'Good. I'll see you tomorrow, then.'

She could be polite and ask him to stay, offer him a drink. But right now she wanted to lick her wounds in private. Though there was something else she needed to know. 'How long was it before you stopped loving Bianca?'

He spread his hands. 'I guess I was pretty hurt and angry when she left. But I was relieved in the end because it meant I didn't have to keep pretending that everything was fine, for her sake. She didn't cope well with the idea of me being unable to walk and needing care. She wanted to be the one who was looked after.'

'Are you friends now?'

'No. I'd be civil if I saw her. And I hope she's happy. But I've moved on. I don't love her any more.' He shrugged. 'And I've got my work. I'm happy.'

'Me, too.' And it wasn't a total lie. Since the competition had started, Polly's world had felt more right than it had in a long time. The self-confidence she'd faked for years was finally real, thanks to Liam and his belief in her.

And wanting more, wanting Liam... Well, it wasn't going to happen.

On Sunday morning, to Polly's relief, Liam behaved as if they hadn't had that fight.

'This week, it's the tango.'

'I love watching the professionals dance the tango,' she said. And one Liam had choreographed three or four years ago—before she'd started dating Harry—had left her feeling decidedly hot and bothered.

'I think you're going to enjoy dancing this one. Piazzolla—who composed a lot of music for tango— said that tango was darkness made light through art. Keep that in mind. It's a dark, sensual dance. You can't smile your way through it, Polly.'

'As long as I don't do what that poor actress did a couple of years back, and look as if I was sucking lemons through the whole routine.'

He grimaced. 'I remember that. I think I'd rather

you smiled through it. Right. We'll start with the walks. Ballroom hold.'

*A dark, sensual dance...* His words echoed in her head and the air suddenly felt charged. She could barely look away from him.

'We're going to do three steps backwards, side and close. Remember it by spelling out the name of the dance—T, A, N, G, O. Slow, slow, quick-quick slow.'

She repeated the letters as he moved her backwards. But this wasn't like the other dances he'd taught her. He was practically surging against her, pushing her backwards—and it made her want to push him back.

His expression wasn't his serious teaching face, either; it was more intense than that. And it reminded her of the tension between them last night, when he'd accused her of still being in love with Harry. And, although she'd outwardly accepted his apology, she was still inwardly smarting about him saying she was wallowing in her situation.

'Again.'

Still pushing her. Still with that hooded look to his eyes. And she wanted to make him as rattled as he'd just made her feel.

'T, A, N, G, O,' she said as he moved her backwards. He spun her a little on the last step, so the word came out as a breathy 'oh', with almost a sexual quality to it; her face heated when she looked at him.

And he wasn't standing up straight, the way he did for the other dances—he was slightly crouching, as if he was ready to have a fight.

Well, she was ready to fight him right back.

'Promenade.' He talked her through it. 'Snap your head to my right. T, A, N, G, O.'

Except on the 'N' she was facing him again. Almost close enough to kiss him.

'Lunge.' He pulled her right arm up, stepping back at the same time so she ended up leaning towards him. As if she were going to kiss him.

'Pull away,' he said softly. 'Arch your back—it's all about the shape.'

As if he were pulling her towards him and she were avoiding his kiss. Even though she wanted it. Which was why her back was arching, remembering the pleasure he'd given her in Vienna. Wanting him, and yet backing away at the same time.

'Back, side, close,' he whispered, shifting his weight again and pushing her back.

The dance was making her feel hot all over. Liam was making her feel hot all over. And they'd barely started training. If he kept this up, she was going to be a puddle of hormones by the dress rehearsal.

And the only way she could get through it and keep her head was to smile.

\* \* \*

On Monday afternoon, after training, she called Liam. 'Shona's got me an audition for tomorrow morning. Sorry. I hoped I'd have more notice for you than this, but can we change the time of my training session?'

'No problem. When's your interview?'

'Ten. So if the morning isn't overrunning, I can probably make it to your studio by midday.'

'That's fine.'

'Have you heard from the Broadway guy about your audition yet?' she asked.

'No, and he's auditioning people in LA this week. So I'll just have to be patient.'

He'd certainly learned all about patience teaching her to dance. 'I'll keep my fingers crossed for you.'

'Thanks. Break a leg tomorrow. And don't wear green—especially not lime green.'

She laughed. 'Sure. See you tomorrow.'

She barely had time to be nervous for the audition. Time seemed to fly by. Shona was in meetings, so she'd gone to the audition on her own, but that was fine. She put on her best smile, answered all the questions as honestly as she could, and told the producer exactly why she loved working with kids on TV.

By the end, she was overrunning by twenty minutes; she texted Liam to let him know she was on her way.

'How was the audition?' he asked when she walked in.

'OK, I think, but obviously it depends on how the other candidates did.'

'When will you hear?'

'Next week.' She bit her lip. 'Though if I don't do better on Saturday than I did last week, I could be resting again anyway.'

'It'll be fine. Just keep practising, keep smiling, keep trying and we'll get there.'

Their training session that afternoon went well, and Polly was surprised to realise how much more confident she felt since she'd been dancing with Liam. He'd made a huge difference to her life in the last few weeks.

She wished she hadn't been so definite about sticking to being just friends; but it was too soon for her. Plus, if their auditions had both gone well, then they would both have new jobs and they'd be thousands of miles apart in a couple of weeks' time. It wasn't fair to expect him to give up his dreams for her and stay in London to be near her; she wasn't sure she could face uprooting herself again now she was settled in her new life; and she still needed to prove to herself that she could make it as a presenter. So she'd made the sensible choice.

Why did it feel like the wrong one?

* * *

On Wednesday, they started their tango routine to Abba's 'Gimme! Gimme! Gimme!'

'I can't believe you're using this music. You taught me to cha cha cha to this,' she teased.

'It's called being inventive,' he said. 'And remember we're telling the story. It's all about theatricality and passion. You have to be a vamp.'

'I can do vampy,' she protested.

He just laughed. 'Vamps don't smile as much as you do.'

Halfway through the session, the camera crew from *Ballroom Glitz* came in to make a video of their training session for the *Step by Step* show. Liam remembered the very first video, how Polly had been a little shy and hesitant. Now, she'd blossomed and was playing for the cameras. 'This week, Liam's encouraging me to be a vamp,' she said.

Ha. She was far too sweet to be a vamp.

And he was really regretting their 'just good friends' stance. But how was he going to convince her to give them a chance, given there was a real possibility they'd soon be thousands of miles apart? He knew she needed security. He couldn't give that to her. So it was best to keep his distance.

'Look, I've got the vampy nail polish. Though I admit I borrowed it from my best friend.' She showed off her blood-red nails, then took off her shoes and wiggled her toes. 'See, look—matching! And I'm so going to buy the lippie this afternoon.'

Her smile and her laughter were both genuine rather than brave. And adorable. And Liam really wanted to pick her up, throw her over his shoulder and carry her to his bed.

Except he couldn't.

Being just good friends was the worst idea they'd ever had.

At the dress rehearsal on Saturday, Polly was in full vamp mode, wearing a black dress with long black chiffon sleeves and a sparkly bodice, teamed with high heels the same rich scarlet as her nail polish. Her hair was slicked back, her eye make-up was dramatic and her lips matched her nails.

'Vampy enough for you?' she asked Liam.

For a moment, what looked like sheer desire glittered in his eyes, before he damped it down. Or maybe she was kidding herself, seeing what she wanted to see.

'Yes, you look vampy,' he said.

So did he, in a black shirt and black trousers with a red tie that matched her shoes. Utterly gorgeous. Especially as he hadn't shaved since the previous morning. It reminded her of that morning in Vienna, when she'd woken in his arms. Desire coiled deep in her belly at the memory.

Worst still, they were drawn to be on next to last, and the more she looked at him, the more she wanted him.

Help.

She wasn't sure whether it was more relief or terror that propelled her to her feet when Millie announced them: 'Dancing the tango to "Gimme! Gimme! Gimme!", it's Polly Anna and Liam!'

The music started, and they went through the routine. Every time she did the head flicks, she was so aware of his mouth passing so near to hers. And there was one place where she couldn't help herself tipping her head back and almost begging for a kiss—which wasn't in the choreography. He noticed, too, because those gorgeous navy blue eyes dilated.

Time stopped.

His lips parted slightly.

She just knew he was going to kiss her…

But then he dragged in a breath and spun her round instead, into the next move.

And somehow the dance had ended and they were standing in front of the judges' table.

Tiki was first to comment. 'Gimmicky use of the chair, you lost your timing and you smiled too much. But it was a definite improvement on last week.'

Praise from Tiki? Unbelievable. And very, very welcome. 'Thank you.' Polly beamed at her.

Robbie fanned himself. 'I always thought of you as the girl next door, Polly Anna, but tonight…' He made tiger hands and growled, making her laugh.

'You obviously enjoyed this one,' Scott said, 'and you were vampy in places. Though I'd like to see more of an emotional connection instead of you smiling your way through the dance every week.'

'Before you two go,' Millie said, 'I have to ask the question on everyone's lips or they'll never forgive me. Are you or aren't you a couple?'

'We're just good friends,' Polly said.

Millie raised an eyebrow. 'We all thought you were going to kiss each other in the middle of the dance floor just then.'

So had she. And she couldn't help looking at Liam. Looking at his mouth. Wanting to feel it moving against hers, teasing her and enticing her and sending her temperature soaring, the way he had when he'd taught her the steps.

'That was all part of the choreography—part of the story we were telling,' Liam said.

'No way.' Millie laughed.

'Yes, way.' He winked at her. 'I'm glad that my choreography's so convincing.'

'Hmm.' Millie didn't sound as if she believed him. 'Well, good luck and we'll wait to hear the scores.'

Even though Polly thought they'd done well and the judges' views had been positive, the other couples had done better. From the leader board, it looked as if they were going to be in the dance off.

'Remember the public vote can save us,' Liam reminded her. 'Hopefully they like us enough to want us back next week.'

Half an hour later, when the public vote was included in the scores, they were all called down to the floor. They stood under the spotlights, as usual. Had she done enough? Polly wondered. Would she have one more week with Liam?

'And through to the semi-finals next week—it's Polly Anna and Liam!'

They'd done it.

They'd actually done it. And they were through to the semi-finals, something she'd never even dreamed would be possible.

She whooped, turned to the camera to thank the public and blow kisses to them, and then kissed Liam swiftly, breaking it off before she made a fool of herself and clung to him. That wasn't part of their deal.

But the public and Liam weren't the only people she needed to thank.

She left the dance floor to where Millie was standing by the judges' table, and kissed all four of them.

Tiki looked completely taken aback; the other three were smiling, clearly loving her enthusiasm.

'I take it you're pleased with the result, Polly Anna?' Millie asked, laughing.

'It's a dream come true. I'm like a dog with—with *three* tails,' she said, beaming. 'Just… Thank you.'

# CHAPTER TWELVE

'It's going to mean a lot of work this week,' Liam said, 'because we're doing two dances on Saturday. Though the good news is that one of them is one we've done before. Would you agree that our best Latin is the cha cha cha?'

'Yes. And it's my favourite dance,' she said. Apart from the waltz, but that wasn't Latin—and also she didn't want to admit to Liam that his highwayman costume sent her temperature up a couple of notches. They'd agreed to be friends. And friends definitely didn't feel that kind of desire for each other.

'We just need to run over the routine a few times to freshen it up, but we know what we're doing there.'

She nodded. 'So what's the new dance?'

'The rumba. Actually, it'll remind you a lot of the cha cha cha, even though it's much slower, because it has several similar movements.' He demonstrated the basic. 'It's similar to the beginning step of the cha cha cha, but repeated with eighth turns. Plus the New York and the spot turns. Ready to give it a go?'

'You betcha.'

On Monday, Amanda came in at their break with coffee and cake, as usual. 'Pol, I can't believe you kissed that toffee-nosed Tiki on Saturday!' She grinned. 'She couldn't have looked more shocked than if you'd told her you'd got a job dancing the lead in *Swan Lake*.'

'Well, I could hardly leave her out when I kissed Millie, Scott and Robbie,' Polly said. 'That would've been mean.'

'Even though she's been so mean to you?'

'It's not personal,' Polly said. 'And I don't have to be mean back to her.' Polly softened her words with a smile.

It was one of the things he really loved about Polly, Liam thought. She always saw the good in others.

He caught himself sharply. *Loved?*

He was really going to have to stop thinking like this. He didn't do love any more. He wasn't going to let himself fall for Polly. Neither of them was in a position for a relationship. Both of them were waiting to hear about new jobs that would take up all their time, and then some. She was still hurting from Harry's betrayal—and she hadn't denied it when he'd accused her of still being in love with Harry.

Plus they'd agreed to keep it sensible.

*You are* not *falling in love with Polly,* he told himself.

'Enough slacking over your coffee, woman. We have a routine to prepare,' Liam said. 'Ready to rumba?'

'Sure.'

That smile could break his heart. And he hated the thought that the end of their time together was getting nearer and nearer. But he couldn't see any way out of this. Not when she was still holding a torch for Harry.

But he forced himself to concentrate on work and took her through some new turns.

This was definitely one of the dances that clicked for her, he thought. Because she wasn't having trouble following the footwork, the way she did for the waltz. She was following every instruction perfectly.

'Well done. You're really getting the hang of this.'

She gave him another smile that widened the crack in the barriers round his heart just a little more. 'I know. I'm so enjoying this, Liam. It's great.'

When the practice session had finished, Polly changed her shoes and switched on her mobile phone. There was the usual volley of beeps, but then Polly looked surprised. 'It's Shona. She has news.'

'About your job?'

'I don't know.' She took a deep breath. 'I'm surprised you can't hear my heart beating, it's that loud—just like it is when we're waiting to hear about whether we've escaped the dance off.'

'Call her and find out what she has to say.'

He noticed that Polly paced the studio as she waited for Shona to answer. 'Shona? It's Polly. What's the news?' she asked.

Liam really was trying not to eavesdrop, but he couldn't help it. Polly was the only one speaking, and the studio was silent otherwise.

'Right.'

He couldn't tell whether she was pleased or disappointed; all he could hear was wariness in her voice. So would she want to celebrate, or would she need to be cheered up?

'When will you have that?'

Hmm. Did that mean she had to wait a bit longer to hear about the audition?

'OK. We're done with training, now, so I'll come and see you. Bye.' She ended the call. 'I'm not quite sure I've taken it in yet, but…' She took a deep breath. 'Liam, I've got the job!'

'Well done.' Before he'd really thought about what he was doing, he picked her up and whirled her round, then set her back on her feet. The next thing he knew, his mouth was on hers and he was kissing her, really kissing her—just like in Vienna. And she was kissing him back. Touch for touch, caress for caress.

When he finally broke the kiss, every nerve-end in his lips was tingling.

'Polly,' he said softly. She looked as shell-shocked as he felt.

She shook her head. 'Liam, this is too risky. We can't do this.'

He was about to argue, but he could see the faint sheen of tears in her eyes. So it was still Harry in her heart? Much as Liam wanted Polly, he knew that pushing her now would mean pushing her away. He needed to give her more space.

'Sorry. Can we pretend that didn't happen?' he asked.

'I think that's a very good idea. I need to see Shona. She's got a contract for me to sign, and they're emailing her a schedule.' She dragged in a breath. 'Apparently we're going to be shooting different sections on different days, so I might need to adjust my training sessions, if that's OK.'

'Sure. Let me know your schedule when you can, and we'll sort your training round it.' He wanted to suggest taking her out for a drink or a meal to celebrate her news, but he didn't dare. Because he knew he wouldn't be able to resist doing something stupid. Like kissing her again until they were both dizzy, and then taking it one step further. Just as they had in Vienna.

\* \* \*

So much for thinking her life was on hold after Harry had dropped the bombshell. Polly had never been so busy in her life. On Tuesday, she had dancing practice with Liam in the morning, and a session at work in the afternoon that spilled over to the evening. She was dog-tired that evening, and almost slept through her alarm the next morning, but still managed to get to the set on time.

Wednesday was a full day's shoot, so she had to fit her training session into the evening. When they finished, at half past nine, Liam looked narrowly at her. 'Did you eat before you came here?'

'I didn't have time,' she admitted. 'I'll eat later.' Though she knew she didn't have the energy even to get takeaway food on the way home. The most she'd be able to manage was a bowl of cereal.

'Not eating isn't good for you, Pol.'

'Don't fuss.'

He sighed. 'I get the strongest feeling that you're not going to bother cooking anything for yourself when you get home, because you look tired enough as it is. I don't want you keeling over on me, so I'm pulling rank—and you're coming upstairs with me, right now.'

A shiver of pure desire ran down Polly's spine. Upstairs. To his flat…

She really had to keep Vienna out of her head.

And Monday, when he'd kissed her. She'd agreed

to pretend it hadn't happened. Though she'd replayed it over and over in her head, feeling every nerve-end come alive at the memories. Wanting him to do it again. But the whole thing still scared her. She had a new job. She was pretty sure he'd get the Broadway job, which meant they'd be thousands of miles apart. In different time zones. How could it possibly work? Better to avoid the heartbreak by being sensible now.

'Move,' he said, shooing her out of the studio and switching off the light.

In his kitchen, he made her sit down and refused to let her help while he put pasta on to boil in a pan, heated through a jar of sauce and threw together a salad.

'Thank you. I appreciate you cooking for me,' she said as he grated the cheese.

'This is hardly cooking. It's not as if I'm even making my own sauce—I'm just chucking things together.'

'It's still appreciated, especially as I know you're busy, too. You're working during the day as well as training with me, doing the choreography for the professional dancers and teaching classes.'

'Don't worry about me,' he said. 'I'm used to this, but you're not used to working a full day and learning new dance moves on top of that. And you're doing two dances this week, which is a tough call in any case.'

She bit her lip. 'Maybe I should've refused the job, or asked if they could wait for me to finish on *Ballroom Glitz*. I'm worried I'm going to let you down on Saturday.'

'You won't let me down.' He waved a dismissive hand. 'And you're enjoying your new job so far?'

'I love it,' she said honestly. 'I'm getting the chance to come up with more ideas for the show, too. Obviously I still miss the *Monday Mash-up* crew, but I like my new colleagues. They've really welcomed me on to the team.'

'Of course they would, Polly—you're lovely, and it takes about two seconds after meeting you for people to work that out.'

She blushed. 'I wasn't fishing.'

'I know.' He gave her an intense look.

She wanted to tell him that he was lovely, too, and they could be so good together. But she knew he wouldn't take the risk, and she didn't want to ask and be rebuffed. Though she'd been the one who'd done the rebuffing, in Vienna, so did that mean she had to be the one to make the next move?

Though, with the hours she'd been putting into her new job and her dancing training, she was physically too tired to think straight.

'Polly, you're practically falling asleep,' Liam said at the end of the meal. 'I'll drive you home.'

'It's OK. I can get the Tube.'

'I know you could, but you're not going to—

you're tired. And don't argue. I have a vested interest in you getting some rest so you're fine for Saturday.'

'Do you want to come up for a coffee?' she asked when he'd parked in the road outside her flat.

'Yes, but I'm not going to because you really need to get some sleep,' he said gently.

True. And it would be better still if it was in his arms.

'Liam...' She reached across to rest her palm against his cheek.

As if he couldn't help himself, he turned his head so his mouth was against her palm, warm and soft and in sharp contrast to the stubble that grazed her fingertips.

And then he took her hand and folded her fingers round the place he'd just kissed. 'Pol, we need to be sensible. Neither of us is in the right place for this to work.' But his face was filled with regret, giving her hope.

'Just tonight,' she said softly.

He shook his head. 'It'll make it tougher in the long run. Complicated.'

She knew he was right. But the rebuff still hurt.

'Thanks for the lift. See you tomorrow,' she said, scrambling out of his car before her expression gave too much away.

On Thursday, Polly had another full day's shoot scheduled, so Liam had cleared the evening for rehearsals. Even though he had plenty to do, choreographing a routine for the professional dancers, he still found himself missing his morning dance session with her. Her smile always brightened his day. It didn't feel *right* not seeing her.

He almost ignored the phone when it shrilled, not really in the mood for talking to anyone. Then he glanced at the display and saw that it was an international number.

He grabbed the phone. 'Liam Flynn.'

'Hey, Liam. It's Barney.'

The Broadway producer. 'Hi.'

'I've finished the auditions now—and I'm delighted to say you've got the job, if you still want it.'

*If he still wanted it.*

On the one hand, it was a huge opportunity: choreographing a new musical for Broadway.

On the other, it was a job that would take him thousands of miles away from Polly.

Or maybe that would be for the best.

'Thank you. I'd love it,' he said.

'Great. I'll have my people be in touch with all the details, and we'll talk soon.'

He'd got the job. So his life was going exactly where he wanted it: his career back on track, and a new challenge to fire him up. Everything should feel perfect.

So why did he have this niggle in the back of his head that something was missing? And why did he have a nasty feeling that he knew exactly what—or, rather, *who*—was missing? It wasn't sensible, but he was finding Polly harder and harder to resist.

If only things could be different.

'Have you eaten tonight?' he asked when Polly came in to the studio.

'Yes, I ate with the crew in the studio canteen.'

'Good. Let's go through the routine.'

He waited until the end of their rehearsals before telling her the news. 'Barney called.'

'You got the job.'

It wasn't a question. Even though she had no idea who he'd been up against and what their experience was, she'd still been convinced that he was the best choreographer and the producer would choose him. She'd believed in him more than anyone else ever had, and it warmed him. 'Yes.'

'Liam, that's fantastic.' His dreams had just come true—and Polly was thrilled for him. She put her arms round him and hugged him. 'I told you so! And I'm so proud of you.'

Yet, at the same time, part of her wished that he hadn't got the job. Or that the job had been in London instead of on Broadway, so he wouldn't be thousands and thousands of miles away from her. Which was selfish and ungenerous of her, and she was cross with herself even for thinking it.

She forced herself to give him her brightest smile.

And hoped that he was so happy about his job that he wouldn't notice she was faking it.

Their time together was coming to the end, Polly thought that night as she curled up in bed. This week could be the last time she and Liam danced together. He'd be off to New York soon—and that would be it. They'd be out of each other's lives.

She hated the thought of never seeing him again.

But the only other way was to take a risk she really wasn't ready for. All her instincts told her that Liam would never let her down; but her instincts had been wrong about Harry. Could she trust them again? Could she make a go of it with Liam?

She knew what she wanted the answers to be. But she just couldn't make that leap of trust that they actually *were* the answers. That she could let herself rely on Liam to be there for her and not hurt her.

The next couple of days were manic. The morning shoot on Friday hit technical problems and overran until mid-afternoon. She barely had time to get to the wardrobe department for her rumba dress—a backless number in shimmering burnt orange, with long sleeves and a split skirt so her steps wouldn't be impeded. And then it was time for training.

The lyrics were so appropriate, she thought as they went through the routine. Liam *did* do something to her. And it felt as if she were dancing through fire. Wanting him, and yet scared to want him, all at the same time. Mixed up.

So the judges wanted to see real emotion from her? This week, they would. Because yes, the rumba was sensual—but it was also sad. All about heartbreak and longing and wanting something she couldn't have. And she could feel that in every step she danced.

'You look amazing,' Liam said softly when he saw her rumba outfit at the dress rehearsal on Saturday.

'Thank you. You look good, too.' It was incredible how a simple white open shirt and black trousers could look so stunning on someone.

They were scheduled to dance their best Latin routine first. Millie introduced them: 'And Polly Anna and Liam are back with the cha cha cha to "Sway"!'

She loved the music, loved the routine, and although her first dance on the show had seemed to last for ever, this one tonight seemed to last for just seconds.

'As fun and entertaining as it was last time,' Robbie said. 'I loved it.'

'You've definitely worked on your hip action,' Scott said. 'And you smiled all the way through it, so you were obviously having fun. Well done.'

Tiki, as usual, was grouchy, but finally said, 'I have to agree with Scott that your hip action is improved. I hope you can keep it up for the rumba.'

'Thank you,' Polly said.

Once she and Liam had changed, they waited in the Green Room with the others until they were called on again.

'And now, dancing the rumba to "You Do Something To Me", it's Polly Anna and Liam!' Millie announced.

Polly pulled out all the stops with the rumba. Harry and Grace could've been sitting in the front row of the audience with flashing neon arrows pointing to them, and she wouldn't have noticed. Her attention was totally focused on Liam, and all the yearning she felt for him was poured into the dance. She was near to kissing him at one point, with both her hands cupping his face.

What would he do if she stepped out of routine and actually kissed him?

But she couldn't lose the competition for him like that. Instead, she did what they'd practised. She dropped her hands and walked away as the last notes of the song died down.

Scott whistled when they stood in front of the judges' table. 'I thought you were the sort to smile through everything and I wasn't sure you could pull this off. But you were very emotionally involved in the dance. You blew me away.'

'It was a joy to watch,' Robbie added. 'Your heart and soul were in it and you were really expressive.

It was a great story and the dance was really in tune with the song. I enjoyed it.'

'The rumba is slow, and everything's magnified. There needs to be chemistry, flexibility and hip action,' Tiki said. 'There were technical flaws—' she ignored the boos from the audience '—but there was lots of chemistry, and lots of emotion.'

And that was it. Tonight, there was no dance off. Tonight, it was all about the public vote combined with the judges' scores.

They couldn't do any more, now. Just wait for the usual half-hour for the phone votes to come in and be verified. As usual, a chart band played a couple of their latest songs and the professional dancers did a couple of routines.

And then it was decision time.

'The first one through to the final,' said Millie, 'is…Lina!'

Polly had completely expected it. The pop singer had been top of the leader board every single week.

'Also through is Bryan!' The TV gardener had been the surprise of the series according to the judges; nobody had expected a middle-aged, slightly scruffy man to morph into a real Fred Astaire type.

'And the last place in the final goes to…' There was a drum roll, and then Polly counted ten seconds of total silence while the producers racked up the tension.

Liam's fingers tightened round hers, as if to say,

'It's OK if we don't get through. You danced your best.'

Please, please, let her be good enough. Let her have one more week.

Millie almost squeaked with excitement. 'It's Polly and Liam!'

Polly clapped her hands to her face. She couldn't quite believe it.

She had one more week to dance with Liam.

And she was in the *Ballroom Glitz* final.

She was the last of the three finalists to be interviewed.

'So how do you feel?' Millie asked.

'Stunned—and so humbled that the public put us through. I'm really going to work hard this week to prove everyone's faith in me.' She blew out a breath. 'If anyone had told me on the very first show that clumsy, geeky Polly Anna Adams was going to make it through to the final, I would never have believed them. I'm just so thrilled.' She hugged Millie. 'Thank you.'

'I'm thrilled for you, too, darling,' Millie said.

'Wait, there are other people I need to thank, too.' She rushed over to the judges, nearly tripping over her skirt, and hugged them in turn. 'And thank you. Your comments have helped, because you've echoed everything Liam's told me. I appreciate your kindness as well as being strict with me.'

This time, even Tiki was smiling. 'Polly Anna,

nobody could ever doubt your enthusiasm and your exuberance.'

Polly smiled back. 'I'll take that as a compliment, because I'm really loving learning to dance and I'm so, so glad I get to do it for one more week.'

Liam was smiling over by Millie. 'I'm glad we get one more week, too. Polly works hard and never gives up. She tries and tries and tries—and she hasn't mentioned a word of it here, but she's got a new job, so she's working full time on that as well as learning to dance. She really deserves her place in the finals. I couldn't ask for a better partner.'

*Me, neither*, Polly thought. *But I just don't have the courage to take that last step. To risk things going wrong.*

# CHAPTER THIRTEEN

THE hectic schedule continued for both Liam and Polly over the next week. Polly couldn't remember ever being so busy and loved every second of it. Liam had choreographed a show dance to incorporate the steps she'd learned over the last two months, plus they were reprising the waltz. She loved their routine and, even though Liam's costume and the fireworks at the beginning of the waltz wouldn't be a surprise, this time, she knew she was still going to enjoy it.

Except on Wednesday morning, just before she started work, Polly had a call from Fliss. 'Pol, I have no idea how to tell you this, but I need to talk to you about something pretty urgent.'

Polly could hear how upset her best friend was. 'What's the matter? Has something happened to Jake or the kids? I can call work and come straight ov—'

'It's not me, Pol, it's you,' Fliss cut in. 'There's a story about you in the press.' She gulped. 'Someone's leaked the story about what happened when you were fifteen.'

Polly went cold. No. It couldn't be.

'It wasn't me,' Fliss said hoarsely.

'Well, of course it wasn't you—you were there for me when it happened. I know you'd never talk to the press about me. You're my best friend, Fliss.'

'Look, I'll call in sick and come straight over.'

'No, don't do that. You can't let the kids down. You've got mock exams this week, and you know you need to be there. If you're not, you'll worry if the supply teacher's doing it the way you would.'

'Are you sure?'

No. Polly wasn't sure at all. She could really do with a hug in person from her best friend—but she wasn't going to be that selfish. 'Course I'm sure,' she fibbed. 'I'll text you and keep you in touch with what's going on, OK?'

'Do that. I'll keep my phone on silent and I'll keep checking it. I'm so sorry, love.'

Polly felt sick as she hung up.

Hardly anyone knew the truth. So who had leaked the story? She knew Fliss would never betray her like that, and neither would Fliss's parents. Her own parents certainly wouldn't do something that would show up their less than stellar behaviour. Her agent wouldn't do anything that would hurt her or wreck her career. The press had stopped vilifying Harry, so he wouldn't have told the press something shocking about her to take the heat off himself—and she didn't think he would've done that in any case. She knew he felt bad enough for hurting her over Grace; he wouldn't have made it worse for her.

Which left...

No. She didn't want to believe that Liam would have betrayed her like that and sold her out to the press. There was no reason why he would do something so cruel. It just wasn't in him.

But then again, how well did she really know the man? They'd worked together for almost two months, but that didn't mean she really knew him. And she'd put her trust in him. Naïve, foolish, whatever—but she'd left herself vulnerable.

This was the result.

She really didn't want to know what people were saying about her, but the sensible side of her knew that she had to face it, and face it fast, so she could start working on damage limitation.

Taking a deep breath, she looked up the stories on the Internet through her phone, and had to bite back the tears. Everything was there, in full detail— even a description of how many cuts were on each wrist. So this story had to be from someone who'd actually seen them.

Again, she didn't want to believe it was Liam, but who else could it be? Looking at it logically, it had to be him.

Oh, help. This was going to cause major trouble

in her job. Kids were impressionable, so any producer on a kids' TV show would worry that some of them might copy what she'd done. Which meant that she'd be out of her new job when she'd barely just started it. And, with a story like this that could be brought up at any time in the future to haunt her, she'd have no chance of getting another job in the field she loved most.

It wasn't just her day job that faced the axe; it would affect the dance competition, too. How could she walk back onto the set of *Ballroom Glitz*? Again, the producers would see what had happened as bad news that would affect the ratings of the show. They'd no doubt talk to her and ask her to walk quietly. She could pretend to be ill and leave the final to just two couples. It wouldn't wreck the show too much, because the first part of the show was a repeat of a routine they'd done before. The producers would simply be down by one dance in each section, and the professionals could step in quickly to fill those slots with a repeated routine.

And if Liam was the one who'd leaked the story—much as she still hated to think it, she couldn't see any alternative—then she didn't want to see him ever again, let alone dance with him.

She couldn't get hold of Shona. In the end she left her agent a voicemail message and a text. *Have seen news. Going to work. Will keep phone on.*

Just as she'd feared, the producer wanted to see

her as soon as she walked onto the set. 'I'm sorry, Polly. We're going to have to let you go.' He gave her exactly the reasons she'd expected, and she didn't have a single argument she could use to counter them. She knew that children's TV presenters had to be squeaky clean, and even though this was ancient history it was still too much for them to handle.

Shona's phone was still busy. Polly placed a call back on the line, and eventually her phone rang.

'Polly? How are you, sweetie?'

'Coping,' Polly said drily. 'And resting again.'

'What? They've let you go? That's ridiculous. I can't believe they haven't let you tell your side of it. They've got the PR machine to use; they could've spun the story and turned everything round. I'm not happy about this at all.'

Neither was Polly.

'I'll put a flea in the producer's ear and see if I can get your job back. Try not to worry, sweetie. Just go home for now; I'll keep you in touch with the situation, and you keep me in touch with any developments, OK?'

'OK.'

Home. Ha. And she was supposed to be at Liam's dance studio, later that day, for their final practice before dress rehearsal.

She couldn't face ringing Liam to say she wasn't going to make it—how could she talk to him, when right now he was her number one suspect as the person who'd torpedoed her life?—and she certainly wasn't going to his studio.

To get into her flat, she had to go in the back entrance of the building; the front door was besieged by photographers who wanted to get a shot of her and reporters who no doubt wanted to hear more gory details from her. Tough. She wasn't talking.

She'd thought that the world had ended when Harry had dumped her, but this was way, way beyond that. And this was one time that her mantra wasn't working. She couldn't make herself smile through this one. Couldn't fake it this time.

Over the day, her phone beeped to signal messages. Fliss, checking in and offering a bolt-hole. Fliss's mum, saying the same thing. Shona, saying she was working on it and to call if she needed to.

And one from her father.

*Why have you let all that business get dragged up again? How can you be so selfish? Your mother's terribly upset.*

*And I'm not?* Polly thought bitterly, deleting the message without replying.

Somehow she needed to sort out this mess.

But right now she didn't have the faintest idea where to start.

Polly was late for training, Liam realised. Really late. From Bianca, he would've expected it. But that wasn't Polly's style. She'd never been late once in all the weeks they'd been working together. Something had to be wrong.

Frowning, he called her.

No answer.

Maybe they'd overrun at work and she just hadn't had the chance to get a message to him. He left a message on her voicemail. 'Polly, it's Liam. Clearly you've been caught up at work. Call me when you can.'

He left it fifteen minutes and called again. 'Polly, I'm worried about you. Ring me.'

He left it another fifteen minutes, then tried her landline in case she'd called in at her flat first. As he'd half suspected, the phone went straight to the answering machine. 'Polly, it's Liam. I'm worried about you. Call me when you can, OK?'

He was about to hang up when he heard a click and Polly said, 'I'm here.'

Her voice was very, very quiet.

'Polly, thank God. Are you all right?'

'Hardly.' She sounded flat and toneless, as if the bottom had just fallen out of her world.

'What's wrong?' Please, don't let her have been in an accident… But no, she wouldn't be at home in that case, she'd be in hospital or something.

'You know what's wrong,' she said, her voice still toneless.

Oh, hell. She sounded just like Bianca. Playing games, flouncing off and not telling him why, expecting him to read her mind. He frowned. He hadn't been a mind-reader then and he wasn't one now. 'I don't have a clue what you're talking about.'

'Didn't Amanda tell you?'

'Amanda hasn't been in today. Her youngest's got a bug.'

'Then why don't you look on the Internet? The story's gone viral.' There was another click, and he realised she'd hung up.

Story? Viral? He still didn't have the faintest idea what she was on about.

He went straight to the Internet and tapped her name into the search engine. A screen came up with story after story listed, most of them entitled *TV Presenter's Shameful Secret*.

He stared at them, horrified to see the précis under each one. It was the story that Polly had barely been able to tell him after he'd seen her scars in Vienna. But what was it doing on the news? He clicked on one story and all the details were there.

It seemed that the story had spread everywhere. All over the social media, and there were some very harsh judgements on her by people who'd never even met her and wouldn't have a clue about the truth.

And there was more recent stuff, too: stories about Polly being sacked from her new job, along with speculation that she'd be thrown off *Ballroom Glitz* at the weekend.

In some respects, it wasn't so surprising that she

hadn't been able to face coming to training tonight. But then again, she'd already told him about this. She knew he wasn't going to judge her about what she'd done when she was fifteen. That he understood. Why hadn't she come to him?

He called her back. 'Polly. I'm so sorry.'

'It's a bit late for sorry, don't you think?' Her voice was still cold and toneless.

He frowned. 'How do you mean?'

She said nothing.

A seriously nasty thought struck him. 'Where did they get this story?'

'You're asking me?'

His blood turned to ice. 'You surely don't think they got it from me?'

Again, she said nothing.

He blew out a breath. 'It wasn't me, Polly. I would never do something so vile to you. I'd never betray your confidence, much less let the press tear you to pieces.' It cut him straight to the heart that she could think that of him. 'I thought you knew me better than that.'

'I didn't want to think you'd done it.'

He supposed that was something.

'But who else could've done it?' she asked. 'I've been over and over it in my head. Shona would never betray me like that; Fliss and her family wouldn't; and my father's already sent me a snotty text today about dragging their names through the mud, so it's pretty clear my parents didn't do it, either.' There was a small sound that sounded like a sob. 'Maybe you didn't mean to do it. Maybe it was an accident, an overheard conversation—but you're the only other one who knows.'

'Well, it wasn't me.' He paused. 'Are you being doorstepped?'

'Of course I am. They all want the gory details.'

He could hear the pain in her voice. And, despite being hurt and angry with her for even thinking that he could do something like this to her, he knew she needed rescuing. And he was the one to do it. 'Pol, I'm coming to get you. I'll call you when I get to the end of your street. Push your way through the mob and just get in the car.'

'Forget it, Liam.'

'Get in the car,' he repeated, 'otherwise I'll come up and break your door down and carry you out to my car, and that will give the paparazzi even more to photograph and the guttersnipes more to speculate about.'

Polly put the phone down, completely confused. She'd thought that Liam had betrayed her, and now he was coming to rescue her.

Or was he?

She couldn't make any sense of today. Just that it hurt. Really hurt.

Her phone rang. 'I'm at the top of the road,' Liam said. 'Get ready.'

She peeped out of the window, just to check—her trust had been so badly dented today, she was going to double-check everything—and she could see a car that looked like his.

*Could* she trust him?

Though she didn't have much choice, if she wanted to get out of here today. And she knew he was perfectly capable of carrying through what he'd threatened.

She locked her front door behind her, strode out of the building, pushed through the gaggle of reporters and ignored their questions.

Liam leaned over to open the door for her. She got into the car and slammed the door, and he drove off.

'I wasn't the one who broke that story, Pol. I really wasn't.'

She could hear in his voice that he was totally sincere.

'And I can't believe you thought I'd do that to you.'

The hurt came through, loud and clear. She'd been unfair to him, blamed him for something he hadn't done. She'd hurt him. Badly. She wrapped her arms round herself, feeling as if she was falling apart and desperately trying to keep herself together.

How did she fix this—any of it?

'I'm sorry I doubted you. I panicked and lashed

out. I shouldn't have done that.' She dragged in a breath. 'I jumped to a conclusion. The wrong one.'

'Everyone makes mistakes.' He still sounded hurt, but she could also hear understanding in his voice.

'So you're not going to hold it against me?' When he shook his head, she sagged in relief. 'Thank you. That's more than I deserve.' She sighed. 'I'm sorry. I couldn't think who else it would be. Not Fliss, Shona, my parents or Harry, and you're the only other one who knew.'

'Harry.' Liam's mouth thinned. 'You didn't mention him before. Why are you protecting him now?'

'I'm not.'

'You're still in love with him, aren't you?'

She looked away, not wanting Liam to see her real feelings. That she was falling in love with someone else—someone who made her feel special and who'd rescued her when she'd needed it, even though she'd hurt him. Someone she knew was attracted to her, but who had so many barriers round his heart that she didn't think she'd ever find a way through to him. 'No.'

'Then why are you so sure it wasn't him?'

'Because I've known him for years.'

'But it wouldn't be the first time he's done something you weren't expecting, would it?'

She cottoned onto his train of thought instantly. 'You mean, like dumping me for someone else, a few days before our wedding? That's true. But what has he got to gain from spreading the story?'

'What would I have had to gain?'

'Nothing. Which is why it didn't make sense. But *somebody* talked to the press.' She sighed. 'I'm sorry. Really sorry. My judgement's rubbish.' She swallowed hard. 'I lost my job this morning.'

'Oh, Pol. That's awful.'

'Children's TV presenters have to be squeaky-clean. I'm not.' She took a deep breath. 'And I think they'll ask me to drop out of *Ballroom Glitz*. I'm sorry. I've really let you down.'

'You haven't let me down at all—and no, they won't chuck you out of *Ballroom Glitz*. Pol, I've been thinking on the way here. You can turn this whole thing around. You don't have to be a victim twice over.'

'My head isn't working straight right now, so can't follow where you're going with this. What do you mean?'

'Whoever spilled the beans obviously did this to hurt you—but, instead of feeling bad about it and letting them get away with it, you can turn it round and make something positive out of it, the way you always do.'

'Smile, you mean?' Because, oh yeah, her heart was breaking right now. This was the time to think of the Chaplin song and give the world her widest smile.

'No, I mean this is your chance to talk about what happened. A chance to give a voice to teenagers who right now are feeling as bad as you did and think they have no way out, just like you did.'

'Talk about it? Where? How?'

'On the *Step by Step* show. Instead of talking about our training this week, you could talk about this. And I'll be there right beside you to hold your hand or do whatever you need me to do.'

Polly was silent for a long, long time while she thought about it. He was suggesting that she should strip her soul bare on national TV. Even the idea horrified her. She'd hidden her scars for so many years; it would be a nightmare to do this. To confess to how low she'd got. How desperate. Relive all the misery.

And yet he had a point. This way, she might be able to help someone else. She might be able to stop them taking the desperate measures she'd taken.

Even though she'd accused Liam wrongly of doing something so horrible, he was still prepared to be by her side. To support her, give her the courage to do it.

It was more than she deserved, and it made her feel like pond life.

'I'll do it,' she said.

'I guess you'd better call Shona and clear it with her, first.'

Polly did so. 'Shona's going to talk to the producer and ring me back,' she told Liam when she'd ended the call.

'Good.'

When Shona rang back half an hour later, Polly said to Liam, 'They want me in the studio tomorrow morning.' She winced. 'What about training?'

'We'll manage—and maybe it'll help, dancing afterwards. Or if you want to go somewhere out of London, that's fine. We'll play it by ear.'

'Thank you. I don't deserve this—not when I doubted you.'

He reached over and squeezed her hand. 'I'm not judging you, Pol. I think my reaction would've been the same. Come on. There's only salad and eggs in my fridge, but I make a mean omelette.'

'I appreciate this, Liam.'

'I know. And it's OK. You'd have done the same for me.'

'Actually, I would.'

He squeezed her hand and let it go. 'I know.'

Her phone beeped with messages almost constantly while she was at his flat.

'I put it through to voicemail—that's why everyone's texting me,' she said. 'Sorry.'

'No worries. Actually, I'm glad you've got so many people looking out for you,' he said.

They managed to dodge the paparazzi later that evening when he dropped her home, and he picked her up in a taxi really early the next morning, knowing that the paparazzi would recognise his car by that point.

Polly felt sick on her way to the studio. She knew she was doing the right thing; but at the same time she was making herself really vulnerable. Her parents would probably never forgive her for this, even though she wasn't intending to go into all the details. And would everyone despise her afterwards, or would her friends—other than Fliss and Shona—understand?

Clearly her worries showed on her face, because Liam hugged her just before they went into the studio. 'You can do this. It's going to be fine.'

'How can it be?'

'Because you're telling the truth.' He held her close. 'I know it's going to hurt, and you don't have to smile through this. It's OK not to put on a brave face.'

'That's how I've coped all these years.'

'I know,' he said softly. 'But you don't have to. You're not on your own, Pol. I'm here by your side, all the way.'

Jessica's face was kind as they walked in.

'Are you all right, Polly?' she asked. 'Can I get you a glass of water or something?'

'Water would be lovely, thanks.' Polly blinked back the tears. Liam was right. She didn't have to smile through this. But at the same time she was terrified that she'd go into meltdown. She couldn't do that. Not until she'd said what she needed to say.

She sipped the water that the runner brought her,

and it helped to calm her. That, and knowing that Liam was right by her side.

'OK. Ready to record in five, four, three, two, one,' the cameraman called.

'You've had a difficult week, Polly,' Jessica, the *Step by Step* interviewer, said, 'with all sorts of stories about you in the press. Thank you for coming here to tell us your side of it.'

'Thank you for giving me that chance,' Polly said softly.

She took a deep breath and pushed her sleeves up to her elbows, then turned her wrists over to reveal her scars. From the corner of her eye, she could see the camera panning in.

'You've always seen me wearing long sleeves on TV, or if I've got short sleeves I'll be wearing gloves or something to cover my wrists—partly because the scars bring back tough memories for me, but partly because I'm ashamed of what I did, and it's really hard for me to show you what I've been hiding. It hasn't been nice seeing the papers gossip about me and speculate, but by telling the truth I can stop all that and reclaim my life. And that's what I'm going to do.'

She was shaking, but hopefully nobody would focus on that. 'As you can see from the scars, I did something very stupid when I was a teenager. I cut my wrists. I was very unhappy, and I didn't feel I could talk to anyone about what was making me unhappy. I couldn't see a way out, and this was the only way I could think of to stop things.' Her throat felt dry and scratchy from holding back the tears. 'It was a cry for help—and, if anyone watching this to-night is feeling that way, I want to tell you now that there *is* a better way of doing things, one that's not going to hurt you as much as this hurt me.' A tear finally leaked down her face, but she didn't brush it away and fake a smile, the way she normally did. Liam was right. It was OK not to put on a brave face. This wasn't about her any more. It was about stopping someone else making the mistake she'd made and taking it too far—and that meant being honest. 'Talk to someone. If you can't talk to someone in your family, or maybe you don't have a family, there's always someone who will listen to you and help you find a way of dealing with the problem. You might have a good friend, or maybe their parents. Maybe there's a teacher or a welfare officer at school, or family doctor, or someone on the end of a telephone helpline who doesn't even know you but knows how to fix problems.' She took a sip of water, and reached for Liam's hand.

Instantly, his fingers tightened round hers, telling her he was there. That she could do this.

'It's hard to admit you can't cope,' she said. 'And it's hard to talk, because you worry that people are going to judge you or despise you or maybe even get you locked up—' fears she'd had for so many years '—but that's *not* going to happen. I've been there. I know how it feels and how hard it is. But you have to take that leap and trust someone, reach out to them for help. Once you've done it and started talking, then things really do start to change. So I'd beg you now, start talking, before you get as desperate as I was. I was lucky. I'm still here. But others…' The words caught in her throat. 'Others didn't make it,' she finished softly. 'Don't let yourself end up like that. Please.'

'Thank you for sharing that with us, Polly. It can't have been easy,' Jessica said.

'It wasn't. Right now it feels as if my whole world's about to go into meltdown. It's hard, facing the past. Facing what I did. I've hidden it for so many years. But if just one person listens to what I said and it helps them, then it's been worth it.'

The camera panned back to Jessica, who gave out the contact details of various helplines. And then, finally, they were free to go.

Liam kissed her very, very lightly. 'Well done. You did brilliantly. Let's get out of here.'

# CHAPTER FOURTEEN

POLLY looked totally drained, Liam thought as they took the taxi back to his place.

'Right. We're playing hooky,' he said when he'd paid the cab.

'What about practising our dance?'

'We've still got tomorrow. I think you need some time out,' he said softly. 'Come on. We're going to the sea.'

He drove her north of London to a small Suffolk seaside town. The beach was almost deserted; they walked for miles barefoot on the sand, and somehow his fingers ended up entangled with hers. They didn't need to talk; just being together was enough. And the swooshing sound of the waves on the shore, the lonely cries of the gulls, were enough to help her get her balance back.

Eventually they sat on the pier eating fish and chips. 'Do you want to go back to London in time to see the show?' he asked.

She shook her head. 'I know I'm a coward, but I can't quite face seeing it on air.'

'You're no coward.' He drew her hand up to his mouth, pressed a kiss into her palm and curled her fingers round it. 'It's going to work out, Pol.'

'Yeah.' She sighed. 'I'd better text Fliss and Shona, so they don't worry about me.'

He noticed that she didn't mention her parents. Thankfully, she didn't mention Harry, either.

When he drove them back to London, she was still very quiet. And, despite the fact she'd been so open and honest on *Step by Step*, the press were still doorstepping her, clearly hoping that she'd let out the last tiny details. He drove straight past.

She stared at him, looking shocked. 'Liam, I thought you were going to drop me off at my flat?'

'Did you see that crowd outside? I can't put you through that. Come back and stay at my place.'

She gave him a wide, wide smile that told him she was really wary about it.

'I have a spare room,' he said softly, 'so this isn't an offer with strings. I can put your clothes through the washing machine and lend you pyjamas and a robe. Obviously they'll be too big, but it's better that than facing that pack of hyenas. You've been through enough the last couple of days.'

She reached over to squeeze his hand. 'Thank you, Liam.'

Back at his flat, he found some clothes for her.

'Have a bath, and I'll put your stuff through the washing machine.'

True to his word, Liam put no pressure on her. He just made her a mug of hot chocolate and made up the bed for her in his spare room.

'Try and get some rest,' he said gently.

'I don't think I'll ever sleep again.' She dragged in a breath. 'Liam, you've already done so much for me. I know I'm being greedy and I shouldn't ask, but would you stay with me tonight and just hold me? Please?'

*She wanted him to hold her.*

And, even though Liam knew she didn't feel the same way about him that he was starting to feel about her—that she wouldn't take a chance on them—how could he push her away?

He'd just have to keep his own feelings out of it. Do right by her. Just hold her, the way she'd asked.

'Sure,' he said softly.

He climbed into bed beside her and curled his body protectively round her, one arm wrapped round her waist; her hand rested lightly on his. Right now, she needed to rest, not talk. No pressure. So he simply lay there, waiting for the tension to leave her body and her breathing to become slow and deep as she relaxed into sleep.

It took a long, long time. But eventually she slept, and he let himself relax into sleep beside her.

\* \* \*

The next morning, he woke first. They'd shifted in the night so her head was on his shoulder and she was sprawled over him—just as she'd been in Vienna.

She'd backed away then.

Would she back away now?

But in Vienna it had been different. In Vienna, they'd made love. Last night, she hadn't wanted that—she'd needed comfort. Kindness. Not love.

A sick feeling coiled in his stomach. Love. Was he crazy? Love didn't work for him. He couldn't feel like that about Polly. He couldn't possibly. Could he? And the more he examined his feelings about her and just how far they'd gone, the more spooked he felt.

He wasn't ready for this. He had a chance to build his career back up, and he wasn't prepared to give that up. And how could he ask Polly to give up her life in London and go with him? OK, so her job wasn't an issue right now, but she'd know nobody in New York, and he'd be spending way too much time at the theatre, putting the dancers through the routines. She'd be lost. He couldn't do that to her.

The last thing she needed right now was pressure or awkwardness. So he'd make sure it was easy for her. Easy for both of them. Gently, he wriggled out of her embrace and left the bed. By the time he'd showered, changed and made sure her clothes from yesterday were dry, she'd woken and padded into the kitchen to find him.

'Thank you,' she said, resting her palm against her cheek. 'For everything.'

'That's what friends are for,' he said lightly, though the words were aimed squarely at reminding himself that he couldn't be anything more to her. 'I was just going to give you your stuff. Help yourself to the bathroom, and I'll make us coffee. And then we have some steps to practise.'

She gave him her brightest smile, and he really wasn't sure how much of it was faking it. But he wasn't going to call her on it. Not today. 'I'll be as quick as I can,' she promised.

After their practice, there was a volley of beeps when Polly turned on her phone. One was from Charlie at *Monday Mash-up.*

*Pol, call me.* ***Urgent****

What was so urgent?

She called him.

'Pol? Are you all right?'

'I'm fine. What's urgent?'

'Harry's resigned as producer. Word is that you're going to get a call from the powers that be, offering you your job back.'

Why would Harry resign?

Then she went cold. It seemed that Liam was a much better judge of character than she was, even though he'd never actually met Harry. 'Was he the one who told them?'

'No.'

Polly's relief was momentary when Charlie continued, 'It was Grace.'

'*Grace?* But how did she know?' She paused as the answer sank in. 'Harry must've told her.'

'She was giving him a hard time about you after he saw you in the show and he was saying how much he regretted hurting you. She thought he'd changed his mind about her and wanted you back. And it looks as if she thought this was the way to stop it, by making you look bad in the press.'

'I don't care if he does want me back—I don't want him back.' She wanted Liam. Though that wasn't going to happen now.

'Danny told her you wouldn't have him back. She obviously didn't listen.'

'They're welcome to each other. I'm moving on.'

'Does that mean you won't come back?' Charlie asked. 'The team isn't the same without you.'

'I'm not sure right now.' She couldn't quite take it in. 'I need some head space.'

'Pol, whatever you decide, we're rooting for you. I wish you'd told us about—well, what happened. We would've been there for you.'

'I know you would, and I'm sorry.'

'We're all voting for you loads of times tomorrow night.'

She laughed. 'You know me. What if I fall over?'

'We don't care. You're a star to us and we love you, OK?'

'You, too.'

There were tears in Polly's eyes when she put the phone down. 'I know now who spread the story,' she said to Liam.

'I was trying very hard not to eavesdrop, but...' He looked rueful and guilty. 'It was Grace, wasn't it? Are you OK?'

'Yes. And I'm sorry again for blaming you. I'm a rubbish judge of character.'

'No, you just trusted the wrong person.'

'Not for the first time,' she said ruefully.

'Everyone makes mistakes.'

'And I've made too many of them. Especially where you're concerned. I'm sorry.'

'It's OK. I understand.'

'Thank you.' She sighed. 'I'd better head over to the wardrobe department. With all this mess, I haven't sorted out my dress yet.'

'Do you want me to go with you?' Liam offered.

Relief flooded through her. She'd been dreading this. 'Would you?'

At the studio, Rhoda hugged her. 'Sweetheart, I knew there was something, because you were so insistent about sleeves. I thought you'd had a car accident or something and had scars you didn't want people to see. You daft girl, did you think anyone would judge you?'

'Well, yes,' Polly admitted.

'Someone as lovely as you, you're a joy to work with. Of course nobody's going to judge you. And if they do, well, their opinion isn't worth anything.'

'I was going to be brave tomorrow and ask for a dress with—' The words caught in her throat, but she forced them out. She could do this. 'A dress with no sleeves.'

Rhoda nodded. 'We can do that.' She waved Liam away. 'Go and sit in the canteen or something. We'll look after her.'

Liam looked at Polly, and she gave him a tiny nod to tell him that everything was going to be just fine.

Afterwards, Liam drove back to Polly's flat. 'It looks as if the paparazzi realise you're not going to play.'

'No.'

'So it's safe for you to go home.'

Polly swallowed hard, pushing the disappointment back. How stupid of her to hope that he'd ask her to stay over again. But she'd already asked a lot of him. She'd asked him to help her face the cameras to tell her story. To hold her while she slept. To go with her so she wasn't alone when she went to the wardrobe department and had to face their reaction. He'd done all that.

Asking for more would be greedy.

Though she had the nasty feeling that he was starting to back away from her again. And she didn't know how to bridge that growing distance.

'See you tomorrow morning. We'll squeeze in one last rehearsal, OK?'

'OK. Thanks—well, for everything.' And this time, she didn't kiss him goodbye. Not even on the cheek. Because she couldn't face watching him put all his barriers up again.

The next morning, at the rehearsal in Liam's studio, Polly was even more sure that he was backing away from her. She spent the time between then and the dress rehearsal veering between misery and anger. And when she missed a step of their show dance in the dress rehearsal and he didn't say a word, anger won.

She stopped dead, ignoring the music. 'How are we going to get through the final when you're not in it heart and soul?' she demanded.

Liam stared at her. 'What? Of course I'm in it heart and soul.'

'No, you're not. You're doing the separate thing again. Backing away from me. And we're not going to be convincing dancing partners.'

'Polly, we haven't got time for this. We need to finish practising.'

She folded her arms. 'When you're being distant? Liam, I thought you—we…' She shook her head, almost growling in frustration. 'You drive me crazy. I must be out of my mind to be in love with you.'

He went totally still. Silent.

And she realised what she'd let slip.

She'd told him what she really felt about him. What had been growing ever since he'd danced with her in that candlelit ballroom in Vienna.

That she loved him.

She loved him?

Did that mean she'd go to New York with him, if he asked her?

Possibilities bloomed in Liam's head.

And then all the memories slammed back in. Of how fresh and bright and happy it had been in the early days with Bianca. How he'd loved her and been so sure she'd loved him. Just like this fresh, bright, happy feeling filling him now.

But it hadn't lasted.

How could he be sure that Polly's feelings wouldn't change?

*I must be out of my mind to be in love with you.*

She didn't sound too happy about it.

He couldn't process this. It was all too overwhelming. He needed some space. 'I can't deal with this right now,' he said, and walked out.

Polly watched Liam's retreating back.

She'd told him she loved him, and his response

was to walk out. He was abandoning her—just as her parents had, and just as Harry had.

She'd been so stupid to think he was her knight on a white charger. Even though he'd rescued her when she'd needed him, it was only a temporary thing. He'd backed away from her. Put all his barriers back up. He was never going to let her close to him. Never going to let himself love her back. And she'd be a fool if she thought he would.

Liam stayed out of Polly's way until the last possible moment, before going into the Green Room dressed ready for their waltz. He was glad of the domino mask; at least it hid some of his face, and hopefully most of his emotions.

But if he thought he'd put barriers up, he had nothing on Polly. He'd had no idea that brown eyes could ever look that icy. And her back was very, very straight.

This wasn't going to be like the sweet, sexy waltz they'd danced in Vienna.

This was going to be more like a tango, simmering with tension and aggression.

One of the runners came up to them. 'You're up now. Ready?'

'Better face the music and dance,' Polly said, her super-bright smile well in place.

*I must be out of my mind to be in love with you.*

Yeah. And he had a feeling that he was out of his.

He forced himself to concentrate on the dance, steps so familiar that he was practically on autopilot. But the words of the song seeped into his head.

So damn true.

He needed someone's arms to hold him tight. He needed someone to tell him when he was lying, especially when he was lying to himself.

And Polly was that someone.

She fitted.

Face the music? Face facts, more like. He needed her. He needed the love she'd offered him and he'd been too stupid to accept.

And he needed to put that right. Right here, right now.

He stopped dancing.

Polly stared at him, looking shocked. 'Liam?'

He glanced over to the leader of the orchestra and put his hand up in the age-old 'stop' signal, and the music faded.

He didn't care that the studio was full of people watching them. He didn't care that it was being broadcast live to millions more. Right now, the most important thing in the world was to tell Polly how he felt. What he'd been too scared to open up and tell her.

He dropped down on one knee.

'I love you, Polly,' he said. 'What you said to me this afternoon...I'm sorry. I didn't know what to say to you. But I know what to say now. You're brave and you're funny and you make my world a much, much better place.' He paused. 'If I had to choose between you and dancing, I'd choose you. Every single time.'

Her eyes went wide. 'But—but dancing's who you are. It's like breathing for you.'

'I'd still choose you,' he said. 'I love you. And I was too stupid to tell you before. Too scared. And I shouldn't have been. Yes, we've got a few things to sort out. But the most important thing is that you told me you love me. And I love you. More than I can say. More than I can dance. I know you hate risks and you don't believe in promises, but I hope I've proved to you that I'll always be here for you and taking a risk with me would be safe. Polly, will you marry me?'

Time seemed to stretch. Thinly enough to let the panic seep through again.

Had he got this wrong? Had he misheard when she'd said she loved him? Misunderstood?

She blew out a breath. 'Playing it safe didn't work out for me. So I'll take the risk, Liam.' She smiled. 'I love you, and I know you love me. We're a good team. Like they said in the film, when it goes wrong, you just keep tangoing, and that's what we can do—because you've taught me how. I love you, Liam, and I'd be proud to marry you.'

He whooped, got to his feet, spun her round and kissed her silly.

Millie tapped him on the shoulder. 'Guys? Hello? We're supposed to be in a dance show? The judges are waiting.'

'Sorry.' But Liam didn't feel in the slightest bit repentant as they followed Millie over to the table. Polly had said yes. Nothing else mattered.

'I don't know what to say,' Tiki said, shaking her head. 'I've never seen anyone propose to anyone in the middle of a dancing competition before. I...er... Well, congratulations!'

'Thank you.' Liam hugged Polly.

'I'm sorry—you didn't finish the dance, so we can't put you through.'

The audience booed.

'It wouldn't be fair to Bryan or Lina,' Tiki said. 'But...well, I guess you have something better than that.'

'I do indeed,' Liam said. 'She said yes.'

'Couldn't you have waited until after the dance to propose to her?' Millie asked, when the cheers had finally subsided enough for her to be heard.

'When you finally decide to take your life off hold, you want it to start that very second—so, no, I couldn't wait,' Liam said. 'And although it would've been lovely to think that we could win a trophy, I think I've won a bigger and better prize than anyone could've ever offered me. Polly Anna Adams, I love you, and you've made me the happiest man in the world.' He kissed her and spun her round again.

The applause, whistles and cheers were deafening.

'You've made me the happiest woman in the world, too.' This time, Polly couldn't hold back her tears. 'And these are happy tears,' she said, her voice wobbly.

'Trust my Polly to smile brightly when she's unhappy and cry when she's happy.' But Liam was smiling as he held her close.

'Sometimes you have to break a rule for the integrity of the dance,' Tiki said, 'and I think we're going to break a rule here. As I said, we can't put you through to the final because it wouldn't be fair to Lina and Bryan—but I for one want to see your show dance.'

'Absolutely,' Scott and Robbie chipped in.

Millie faced the audience. 'Do you want to see them dance?' she asked.

There was a resounding cheer of 'Yes!'

'What do you think, Pol? Ready to put on the glitz?' Liam asked.

She smiled and kissed him. 'With you Liam, *always*.'

\* \* \* \* \*

# LARGER-PRINT BOOKS!
## GET 2 FREE LARGER-PRINT NOVELS PLUS
## 2 FREE GIFTS!

**HARLEQUIN®**

*Romance*

### From the Heart, For the Heart

---

**YES!** Please send me 2 FREE LARGER-PRINT Harlequin® Romance novels and my 2 FREE gifts (gifts are worth about $10). After receiving them, if I don't wish to receive any more books, I can return the shipping statement marked "cancel." If I don't cancel, I will receive 6 brand-new novels every month and be billed just $4.59 per book in the U.S. or $5.24 per book in Canada. That's a savings of at least 20% off the cover price! It's quite a bargain! Shipping and handling is just 50¢ per book in the U.S. and 75¢ per book in Canada.* I understand that accepting the 2 free books and gifts places me under no obligation to buy anything. I can always return a shipment and cancel at any time. Even if I never buy another book, the two free books and gifts are mine to keep forever.

119/319 HDN FVSK

| Name | (PLEASE PRINT) | |
|------|------|------|

| Address | | Apt. # |
|------|------|------|

| City | State/Prov. | Zip/Postal Code |
|------|------|------|

Signature (if under 18, a parent or guardian must sign)

### Mail to the **Harlequin® Reader Service:**
**IN U.S.A.:** P.O. Box 1867, Buffalo, NY 14240-1867
**IN CANADA:** P.O. Box 609, Fort Erie, Ontario L2A 5X3
**Are you a current subscriber to Harlequin Romance books**
**and want to receive the larger-print edition?**
**Call 1-800-873-8635 or visit www.ReaderService.com.**

* Terms and prices subject to change without notice. Prices do not include applicable taxes. Sales tax applicable in N.Y. Canadian residents will be charged applicable taxes. Offer not valid in Quebec. This offer is limited to one order per household. Not valid for current subscribers to Harlequin Romance Larger-Print books. All orders subject to credit approval. Credit or debit balances in a customer's account(s) may be offset by any other outstanding balance owed by or to the customer. Please allow 4 to 6 weeks for delivery. Offer available while quantities last.

**Your Privacy**—The Harlequin® Reader Service is committed to protecting your privacy. Our Privacy Policy is available online at www.ReaderService.com or upon request from the Harlequin Reader Service.

We make a portion of our mailing list available to reputable third parties that offer products we believe may interest you. If you prefer that we not exchange your name with third parties, or if you wish to clarify or modify your communication preferences, please visit us at www.ReaderService.com/consumerschoice or write to us at Harlequin Reader Service Preference Service, P.O. Box 9062, Buffalo, NY 14269. Include your complete name and address.

HRLP13

The series you love are now available in

# LARGER PRINT!

The books are complete and unabridged—
printed in a larger type size to make it
easier on your eyes.

**HARLEQUIN** *Romance*

From the Heart, For the Heart

**HARLEQUIN**
**MEDICAL**™
*Pulse-racing romance,
heart-racing medical drama*

**HARLEQUIN**
# INTRIGUE
**BREATHTAKING ROMANTIC SUSPENSE**

**HARLEQUIN** *Presents*

*Seduction and Passion Guaranteed!*

**HARLEQUIN** *super romance*

*Exciting, emotional, unexpected!*

Try **LARGER PRINT** today!

Visit: www.ReaderService.com
Call: 1-800-873-8635

**H HARLEQUIN**®

A *Romance* FOR EVERY MOOD™

www.ReaderService.com

HLPDIR13

# *ReaderService*.com

## Manage your account online!

- Review your order history
- Manage your payments
- Update your address

---

*We've designed
the Harlequin® Reader Service
website just for you.*

---

## Enjoy all the features!

- Reader excerpts from any series
- Respond to mailings and special monthly offers
- Discover new series available to you
- Browse the Bonus Bucks catalog
- Share your feedback

*Visit us at:*
**ReaderService.com**